The Passover Saga
Myth or History?

Aaron Kolom

PublishAmerica
Baltimore

© 2010 by Aaron Kolom.
All rights reserved. No part of this book may be reproduced, stored in a retrieval system or transmitted in any form or by any means without the prior written permission of the publishers, except by a reviewer who may quote brief passages in a review to be printed in a newspaper, magazine or journal.

First printing

This is a work of fiction. Names, characters, places, and incidents either are the product of the author's imagination or are used fictitiously. Any resemblance to actual persons, living or dead, events, or locales is entirely coincidental.

PublishAmerica has allowed this work to remain exactly as the author intended, verbatim, without editorial input.

Hardcover 978-1-4560-0162-9
Softcover 978-1-4560-0163-6
PUBLISHED BY PUBLISHAMERICA, LLLP
www.publishamerica.com
Baltimore

Printed in the United States of America

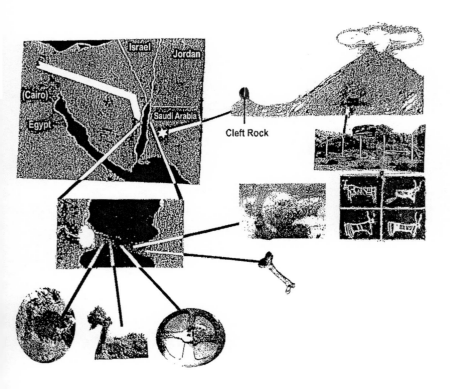

Map of Exodus route – from Egypt, across Sinai Peninsula to Gulf of Aqaba; to expanded view of under-sea ridge-path – artifacts strewn along path: coral-covered chariot wheels and bones of horses and men; to cleft rock; to Mt. Sinai, altars at base (in barbed-wire enclosures) with drawings of Egyptian Apis bulls (all Internet verifiable).

Contents

I
Circa 1300 BC, Egypt;
the Royal Palace of Pharaoh Dudimose
(36ᵗʰ Ruler, 13ᵗʰ Dynasty)

As Binami, lying flat on the gallery floor, peered down through the open weave of the curtains onto the Throne Room below, he carefully shifted his position, holding his breath lest the slightest billowing of the drapes catch the eye of a guard. Had they noticed anything? Apparently not. He quietly exhaled as he leaned his head against the railing. If discovered, it would certainly mean banishment despite being a Prince of the Royal House, possibly even torture and death.

It had been a long afternoon. Manthro, his old teacher and mentor, had secretly told him where to hide to watch the second meeting of Moses—accompanied by the priest, Aaron of "Bnai Israel", the children of Israel or Hebrews— with Pharaoh. The palace had been abuzz with rumors of a Hebrew slave revolt, led by Moses, since his return to Egypt after a great many years—some said, having been forced to flee in fear for his life. Palace whispers were that Moses had been a Royal Prince and army commander to Pharaoh Sobekhotep some forty years before; Manthro, having been Royal Chronicler to Pharaoh at the time, told Binami that it was Moses' popularity as a victorious military leader that had enraged the jealous monarch, causing Moses to flee Egypt in fear. Moses had now returned, white-bearded but still vigorous, taking over as leader of the Hebrew slave peoples, together with their chief priest, Aaron, said to be Moses's blood brother and older. It was also claimed that Moses had mysterious powers from his strange god, Jehovah.

Manthro, after being Royal Chronicler to two pharaohs, had been replaced by Pharaoh Dudimose, becoming teacher and mentor to young princes like Binami, even the Crown Prince Tutankhamen. Still interested in palace politics and government affairs, Manthro had told Binami of the first meeting of Moses and Pharaoh, that Moses had demanded the Hebrews be set free to worship their own god—with Pharaoh reacting with rage, ordering Moses to leave, and that the daily tasks of the Hebrews would now be increased. From now on, Pharaoh had thundered, the straw for the daily quota of bricks would have to be gathered by the slaves themselves. The outcry from the Hebrews was heard everywhere, leading to this, the second meeting.

For more than twenty years together, as teacher and pupil, neither having family members in the palace, Prince Binami and Manthro had grown close, like father and son— yesterday, Manthro had said he would soon tell Binami about his own personal background, how he came to be an Egyptian Prince, although of lower caste, without royal rank.

As the afternoon shadows lengthened over the courtyard, Binami looked for the slave girl he often dreamed of, Lansel, who gracefully carried urns of water for her mistress's bath about this time of day. They had never been alone together, never even spoken, but over the years now, each had become aware of the other, excitement sparkling each other's countenances as their eyes would meet.

Binami became quickly alert as guards and palace officials began arriving. Although too far away to understand normal conversation, Binami could clearly see the area in front of the royal throne: Moses and Aaron were led in by guards, but kept at a distance from the raised and empty thrones. Moses, though white-bearded, was tall and strong-looking, Priest Aaron was somewhat shorter and of slighter build, but both stood taller than the Egyptians. Moses carried a long shepherd's staff, a crook at the top.

Crown Prince Tutankhamen entered the room, accompanied by officials and guards—striding to a secondary small throne, but remaining standing. Then came Pharaoh, his Vizier at his side, then a phalanx of guards, spears at the ready. Behind the guards were Egyptian priests of the God Ptah, robed in white. As Pharaoh sat down on his throne, Prince Tutankhamen also sat—everyone else remained standing.

Binami saw the Vizier point, heard his voice, but could not make out words.

Then he saw Moses's face darken, heard his voice, angry, though his speech was halting, then Moses gave his staff to Aaron, who threw it onto the floor. A gasp of alarm arose as the staff seemed to become a snake, writhing and slithering across the floor. The guards quickly stepped in front of the thrones, spears poised.

At a sign from Pharaoh, three Egyptian priests came forward, throwing down their staffs, which also became writhing snakes. Another gasp from everyone, including Binami, as Moses's snake, one by one, devoured the priests' snakes.

Pharaoh stood up, clearly enraged, imperiously pointing to Moses and Aaron. The guards lowered their spears and charged the two Hebrews, forcing them outside—but before they left, Moses reached down and picked up his snake—which again seemed to be only a shepherd's staff.

Pharaoh stomped out of the chamber, followed by everyone. Binami watched, unmoving, until the room became empty. Still he remained motionless, until all but one wall torch had burned out. He then, unseen, climbed down and swiftly went to Manthro's room where he knew he was being anxiously awaited.

Manthro drew Binami into the rear of the room so their whispers would not be overheard. Quickly Binami told what he had seen. Manthro was familiar with the Egyptian priests magical trick with rigidized snakes, but pressed for details about Moses staff becoming a snake—which then devoured the others before everyone's eyes—then again becoming what seemed to be a wooden staff.

Manthro sat silently, thinking. Binami respectfully, was also quiet. Then Manthro told Binami what he should do the next morning.

"The god of the Hebrews must be very powerful, so this is not the end. You must be at the slave quarters tomorrow at dawn where you can see and follow Moses." Then, in hushed tones he told Binami what he had promised: about the time when Egyptians, fearful of a slave revolt, killed off Hebrew male babies; about a daughter of Pharaoh rescuing

Moses from the Nile, adopting him and raising him as a Royal Prince and an acclaimed military commander—then having to flee for his life to the land of Midian.

Then, said Manthro, "You, Binami, like Moses, were a Hebrew male infant, destined to die, but like many others, were floated in a basket on the Nile by hopeful mothers— that someone would find you. While you were fortunate and were saved, your rescuer was an unmarried aunt of Pharaoh—so you became a prince, but not a Royal Prince like Moses."

Binami sat quietly, absorbing the knowledge that he was not Egyptian but a Hebrew by birth, and lucky to be alive and raised in the royal palace—that he had not been killed or made a slave. One thought however, crept into his mind, the slave girl Lansel—this meant what? Could they now, perhaps, have a life together? On that exciting thought, he finally slept.

Ia

Circa 2000AD, Study Group: Ancient Customs, Pre-Recorded-History (Canaan—Israel)

The group of 21st century scholars, in informal eMails, Tweeters or textings, referred to their once-a-month "fun-research" get-togethers as "C2C"—from "Conflict-to-Confirmation"—follow-on to "Science versus Bible" and "The Passover Saga—Myth or History?" Each individual's religious belief or disbelief was not a factor —whether the Bible was truth or story—most of them probably retaining a bit of childhood religious teachings. But even if so, it was not the "forcing function"—the appeal for the post-doc meetings was intellectual, like puzzle-solving, irrefutable facts and logic, mysteries being unraveled—iconoclastic knowledge was the excitement and goal.

As a group, all respected each other's religious beliefs—there was no prying, no patronizing, no proselytizing. They all found intellectual stimulation in the ever-forward march of science, the excitement in establishing 'truths' in humankind's history of attained knowledge—occasionally reversed—or modified—or verified.

They were a mixed bag, scholars in various field specialties. What they had in common was being ex-graduate students of Professor Zacharias Henri Barrett, Archaeologist and Egyptologist. Now they gathered on the third Thursday evening of each month, at the professor's home in Westwood, California—refreshments: his coffee, tea, cookies or beer. The set-up and atmosphere was casual, congenial, collegial. For each session, the professor would select a subject and presenter, but all members were required to feed research items to both professor and presenter, the latter to combine them into a power point layout presented on an overhead projector; the format was crisp, succinct, minimum verbiage and factual. Armchairs and sofas were distributed around the coffee table, making a relaxed atmosphere. During the presentation, comments by anyone were expected.

The pets and "babies" of the group—all others being in their thirties to fifties—were Bethe and Avi, a late-twenties couple; Bethe, a math PhD, was the spark-plug, with dynamic infectious zest (causing the others to chuckle with pleasure as she "lit up" on a subject, both hands sweeping her thick, curly hair back from her face); Avi was reserved, a Quantum Mechanics Physics PhD— they had found each other through Professor Barrett's class. Both were deeply religious Jewish, with formidable knowledge in Talmud and Torah, the interest here, for them, as for all the others, was neither piety nor ideology, but scientific fact and logic, the pure pleasure of intellectual discovery.

Then there was Ranah, an Environmentalist PhD researcher at a Fortune 500 corporation; Stewart, MD and PhD medical researcher, working for a pharmaceutical company; Lanit, a Physician's Assistant with a strong penchant for Archaeology; Laurence, Patent Attorney; and Serah, a trial lawyer, with an inclination to the unusual. They were the regulars; attending when they were in town were Dana, an Investment Banker and Rick, a political speech-writer.

It had started as a class project—originally there were a score, now dwindled to eight or nine, not counting the professor; married or single or divorced, man or woman—the "fun" was their discoveries. Nowadays, computer research with the Internet or "web" was simple. No more of remote, dimly-lit libraries, and musty heavy tomes on dusty shelves,—now, effortless keyword queries produced dozens of reference items—and with pictures.

Professor Barrett looked forward to these sessions with his post-doc students, all enjoying the stimulating scholarly atmosphere of debate and discovery. Retired from a lifetime of academic pursuits under the auspices of UCLA, he and his student-colleagues had settled into the subject as a sort of group hobby. With all having "day jobs" at successful careers in various fields, they occasionally joked about putting out a collective book—whether or not the biblical narrative was fictional or a mostly-true history of ancient times. Someone had even nailed down, "Science versus the Bible—From Conflict to Confirmation" at the Copyright office—just in case.

The thematic genesis of the subject had evolved from a philosophical discussion about early civilizations—the pre-recorded history period. Bethe had observed that there seemed to be consistent similarities in societal and cultural development versus biblical stories - solid evidence from thousands of clay tablets, tending to corroborate almost-identical biblical narrative. Avi contributed examples of tablets describing practices and customs of early human-relationships which paralleled biblical tales. Soon all were contributing. The subject was continued— Bethe, to be the presenter.

Professor Barrett opened the next session with an observation about Bible and "history"—that, while the predominant view during past centuries had been to dismiss the Bible as myth, during just this last half-century, numerous archaeological findings had reinstated its importance as credible history.

Quoting the eminent British historian, Paul Johnson, "[I]n Palestine and Syria, investigations of ancient sites and translations of a vast number of legal and administrative records, have tended to restore the value of early biblical books as historical narrative." Also, "Whereas fifty years ago, an early passage from the Bible was generally assumed to be mythical or symbolic, the onus of proof has now shifted; increasingly scholars now must assume that the text contains at least a germ of truth."[156]

The professor nodded to Bethe, who stood up, turned on the overhead projector, placed some papers on it, then, with both hands, swept her thick hair from her face. She smiled a "Hi" to everyone and began: "There have been so many tablet-records of millennia ago, recently discovered and translated, which depict early communal life—and which add credibility to biblical narrative as representing true historical documentary. It is that richness of biblical detail," Bethe emphasized the words, as her eyes sought out the audience, one by one, "which imply actual occurrences—there's a 'ring' of veracity to many biblical stories when compared to ancient tribal customs during man's cultural development. Archival evidence from cuneiform records of the earliest city-type communities show remarkable similarities with biblical tales."

Bethe then put up the power point data, reading the highlights:

• "Archaeological digs at Ebla and Mari: 14,000 tablets were found at Ebla in northern Syria, and 22,000 at Mari, north of the Syria-Iraq border. These archival tablets from the 3rd and 2nd millennia BC, explain events and cultural customs which are consistent with many previously obscure biblical passages."[163]

• "Land purchase: burial plots bought by a stranger who moves into a community—requiring agreement by the local leaders to such alien newcomer acquiring land; a ritualistic ceremonial negotiation over price was required; then there was a formality of witnessing the weighing and transfer of coins; then the recording of the event." Bethe looked around the group, "The biblical description of Abraham's purchase of the burial plots at Machpelah in Hebron, Israel, and the extensive detailed description of the elaborate and drawn-out courtesies of negotiation, are in perfect accordance." [157] Bethe smiled at Avi, who gave her a thumbs-up as she continued.

• "Murder, revenge and safe-haven-cities: in the story of Cain and Abel, the phrase, 'Am I my brother's keeper?' are such powerful words, they just indicate credibility re historical veracity—a reflection of community-rejections of murder—plus the establishment of haven cities where a fleeing 'killer', would find protection from any vengeful kinfolk of his victim." [158]

• "Tablets at Nuzi, dated 1600 BC, parallel Abraham's dealing with a domestic situation—his wife Sarah being childless, and his taking as concubine, her maid-servant—Hagar," Bethe raised her eyebrows as she spoke, while Stewart muttered, "Great custom." Bethe continued, "Hagar then has a son, and, like these extra-biblical records, the Bible describes Abraham getting into inheritance rights—then later, there is a subsequent birth of his son, Isaac, to his real wife Sarah."[164]

• "Noah-type floods: Although the biblical story of Noah and the Flood is based on a God-man morality theme, hard evidence is now available of a world-altering deluge followed by massive land inundation—about four millennia BC—" Bethe acknowledged the general nodding of heads,

"—and with a Noah-like figure and a large ship. Cuneiform tablets describing such a flood and personage were found in 1850 in the Palace of Sennacherib, later confirmed by additional tablets found in a second palace.[159] Also, alluvial evidence of a flood was found at Ur, dated to 4000-3500 BC, and two tablets in the British Museum refer to a large boat." She took a breath, then continued. "The Sumerian story of Gilgamesh is the earliest version of a flood, dated at four millennium BC."[160]

• "Ziggarat Tower," Bethe shrugged, "it's a bit much to accept the Bible story of the Tower of Babel—God causing the diversity of languages to prevent a tower from reaching the heavens, but a Ziggaret Tower was actually discovered by archaeologist Wooley, dated at two millennia BC."[161]

• "Ur, an ancient Sumer city—was excavated in the 1920's, and is described in the Bible as the birthplace of Abraham."[162]

• "Tablets explaining the deception by the chief of a large family-tribal clan which settles in a kingdom—and telling its ruler that his beautiful wife is his sister—really hits me—" Bethe paused,

"—twice, in the Bible, Abraham claims Sarah is his sister, not his wife—which implies an unflattering cowardice. However, the tablets indicate there was wisdom to it—as the sister to a tribal head, she would have greater legal status and protection."[165]

• "Tablets describe the custom of, and the hierarchy for, carrying on a deceased's person's name,—" Bethe paused, "—this is such a wonderful story, favorite to me and to many —the story of Ruth and Boaz—about the responsibilities and marriage obligations to a widow, by kinfolk of the dead husband."[166]

• "A Nuzi tablet tells of the selling by a first son of his legal birthright—like Esau, in the Bible, selling his birthright to Jacob for a bowl of lentil soup."[167]

• "Nuzi archives also explain a complex relationship of a man adopting his son-in-law as his son—and later having sons of his own—just like Laban and Jacob."[168]

• "Death-bed blessings: a Nuzi tablet tells of the binding significance of an oral death-bed blessing—like Rebecca and Jacob, in the Bible, trying to deceive the dying Isaac."[169]

• "Nuzi tablets tell the importance of 'family gods' as deeds of title, such as 'Nashwi's son shall take Nashwi's gods.'—which explains the significance behind the biblical reference to Rachel stealing Laban's gods —as revenge for his behavior."[170]

17

• "Mari tablets confirm that covenants were solemnized by the legal ritual of slaughtering an animal—as in the Bible, Abraham sacrificed an animal after making his covenant with God, and also by Abraham and Abimelech, after their settling of a dispute over the digging of a well."[171]

• "Archival tablets found in various archaeological 'digs' list individuals with patriarchal-type names, and also actual biblical figures such as Abram, Jacob, Leah, Laban, Ishmael."[172]

As she finished, Bethe heaved a sigh of relief, Avi grabbing her hand and pulling her down next to him on the sofa, kissing her on the cheek.

"Good job" said Ranah. "Well done" said the professor, clapping his hands, the others joining.

"OK", said Professor Barrett, looking over the group, "shall we continue along this line?" Everyone nodded affirmatively. "Fine—" he said. "—let's move on. There's always been a real problem in disentangling the many Pharaohs of ancient Egypt. Who wants to tackle it?"

Avi raised his hand. The professor nodded in agreement. "See you all in a month."

(Note: Reference numbers are from Brainwashed* and Miracles**, book by author.)

Ib
Circa 2000 AD, Study Group: Disentangling 300 Pharaohs; The Story of Joseph

The next session was opened by Professor Barrett with a verbal sketch of the millennia-long and rich history of ancient Egypt, with its wealth of historical data encompassing both the periods before and after the sojourn and exodus of the biblical Hebrews. He emphasized the tremendous amount of Egyptian artifacts, records and sarcophagi, which made, he said, the main problem being the sorting out of the 300 dynastic Pharaohic rulers. "Avi," he said, "will explain the recent progress made in that regard, but first, I want to introduce a somewhat shameful and delicate subject among historians." The professor paused, all eyes were on him, a puzzled look on many faces.

"Sometimes," the professor continued, "as we go about unraveling past centuries of ancient lands, objectivity can be lost due to either over-desire or hostility—and we have an unfortunate story to tell, which actually involves both elements." He looked at Avi, who nodded affirmatively.

The professor continued, "Archaeologists of the last century, religious Victorian-Christians, were apparently over-anxious to establish an Archaeology-to-Bible link—so they proclaimed the Egyptian Pharaoh Shoshenk to be Pharaoh Shishak of the Bible. That was the first error, caused by over-zealousness and religious fervor. The second error came when this placed Kings David and Solomon, his temple, and the walled-city of Jericho, into the period of Iron Age 11A—known to be lacking in the cultural richness and sophistication as described in the Bible and needed for the building of the Temple. This second error—still very much believed by anti-Semites today—came from so-called 'minimalists' of the present-day Scandinavian School of Archaeology, who extrapolated that error—their scholarly objectivity probably blinded by hatred of Jews—to then proclaim that this proved the Bible to be historically incorrect, and, at best only an exaggeration." The professor then gestured to Avi, inviting him to take over; he then settled himself into an armchair.

Avi strode to the lectern and projector with a sheaf of papers. "OK," he said, "fortunately, during this past decade, we've had the doctoral thesis of David Rohl, a British Egyptologist, whose 'A Test of Time', and his subsequent book 'Pharaohs and Kings', corrected that first error; thus the second also, and eliminated many kinks in the previously accepted sequence and dating of Egyptian Pharaohs. I'll get into how he did this in a minute, but to dispel the previous errors, Rohl proved that Ramesses II was Shishak, the Conqueror of Jerusalem, which placed Kings David and Solomon in the Bronze age, with its rich cultural and cosmopolitan character —completely compatible with the Bible. This revised dating—what Rohl calls his 'New Chronology!— revises the entire chronology of Egypt's Third Intermediate Period." [175]

Avi selected a paper and projected it on the screen. "What Rohl did, was not only to correct erroneous information about Hebrews and Egypt—which had been the conventional view for over a century—but he also established a solid basis for present-day archaeological-historians. The discoveries and analyses by Rohl and his colleagues were based on numerous dating methods, disentangling incompatibilities and sequences, and correcting errors of up to three centuries in the conventional chronologies of over 300 Pharaohs:"[174]

• "Celestial event dating—using retro-calculations of recorded events such as solar eclipses and sightings of Venus, noted as occurring during the lives or at the deaths of certain Pharaohs—which provided independent and precise dating of known rulers:"[176]

• "Burial vault excavations, especially the notations on, and the locations of, heavy sarcophagi, relative to each other in crowded tombs;"

• "Sacred Aphis bull burial data";

• "Records of the Royal Architects";

• "Amarna letters";

• "Stelae."

"It's really amazing," said Avi, "how such wealth of data from so many disparate sources now dovetails so well with biblical narrative—like a jigsaw puzzle coming together. For example, Amarna letters, which 'flesh out' the biblical stories of King Saul; and young David, when he was leader of a mercenary army of 600 men under the aegis of King Achish of Gath—outlawed by Saul; and even adding input about the deaths of Saul's sons."

Avi shifted to another page, projecting it on the screen. "I'm going into the story of Joseph now—" he said, "—truly a remarkable figure in Jewish history. Joseph is the beginning of the Passover story—and surprisingly, also has tremendous significance in Egyptian history." Several of the group shifted their positions for greater comfort, or got themselves a drink, then settled back.

Avi continued. "A morality issue can be found in every episode of Joseph's life: a cocky teen-ager, he is sold into slavery by jealous brothers; imprisoned due to false charges by the wife of his master; overcomes imprisonment to eventually rise to great personal authority and power; saves Egypt and neighboring countries from starvation, including his own people, the Israelites. The story of Joseph in the Bible is easily justifiable as morality fiction. However, as Rohl notes in his thesis, the finding of much extra-biblical evidence, even an actual statue—which I'll go into in a minute—at Avaris of a white-faced, non-Egyptian Vizier, who, by Egyptian records, saved Egypt from a terrible famine—everything fits perfectly with the Bible."

Avi took a sip from a glass of coke, then continued. "In the Bible, after Joseph becomes Pharaoh's Vizier, he is followed to Egypt by his brothers and their families. That sets the stage, centuries later, for the well-known Passover-Exodus stories: Hebrews are subsequently enslaved; Moses, at birth, is saved from the drowning fate of male babies; Moses, as an adult, is forced to flee to Midian; he returns forty years later; and finally, we have the Exodus story, with plagues and miracles and mass deaths of Egyptians—", he smiled at Bethe, then looked at each of the others with a bemused expression, "—and all aspects of the story now have solid extra-biblical corroboration."

"There is an attempted seduction of a young man by a high official's wife, his rejection of her, her false charges and his subsequent imprisonment and release—told in an Egyptian papyrus dated 1225 BC.—identical to the story of Joseph and Potiphar's wife." [178];

"Then there is Joseph, the Vizier and Savior of Egypt: Archaeological digs along the Nile, provide a clear and remarkable corroboration of the biblical Joseph. An unusual life-sized statue—of Imhotep, a non-Egyptian, found at Avaris by Rohl, honors the legendary Vizier, who—by Egyptian—as well as biblical legend, as Joseph—saved Egypt and neighboring peoples from a terrible famine. The statue depicts a white, clean-shaven Asiatic man with unusually-shaped and red hair." Avi added, "And since legend is frequently based on fact, on adjacent Egyptian wall murals can be seen drawings of Asian caravans of the time, with similar-featured, non-Egyptian men wearing multi-colored coats!"[179]

The subject for the following session was selected as, "Was Biblical Joseph the Egyptian Imhotep—the Achiever of Egypt's Wealth?" When Stewart announced that as a medical student, he had become a member of the Imhotep Society, he was the obvious choice of Researcher-Presenter.

Ic
Circa 2000 AD, Study Group: Was Biblical Joseph the Egyptian Imhotep—Achiever of Egypt's Wealth?

After a welcoming comment by Professor Barrett, Stewart walked to the lectern, turned on the projector, and began:

• "The Roman-Jewish historian, Josephus, quotes the writings of Manetho, an Egyptian historian, as follows: 'During the reign of Pharaoh Djoser, 3rd Egyptian dynasty, lived Imhotep… with a reputation among Egyptians like a Greek God'; Manetho even wondered whether Imhotep had been an actual person, because of his outstanding qualities and talents, 'like none other in the history of Egypt.'" [184]

• "On the foundations of the Step Pyramid in Sakkara is carved the name of Pharaoh Djoser and 'Imhotep, Chancellor of the King of Lower Egypt, Chief under the King, Administrator of the Great Palace, Hereditary Lord, High Priest of Heliopolis, Imhotep the Builder…'"

• "The Bible tells of Pharaoh honoring Joseph with much the same offices, 'Thou shalt be over my house'; Pharaoh gives him his seal ring; 'I have set thee over all of Egypt'." [185];

Stewart paused. "So we have an exceptional personage in Egyptian history whose description matches biblical Joseph. Dr. Lennart Moeller, an eminent Swedish Medical doctor and Egyptologist, wrote a book, 'The Exodus Case', wherein he presents tremendous evidence that biblical Joseph can only be the Egyptian Imhotep, the Vizier to Pharaoh Djoser, who, by Egyptian records, saved Egypt and all the neighboring peoples—naturally also, the Hebrews—from famine. To achieve this—we have the evidence of the immense granary storehouses—achievable only by outstanding administrative authority and discipline—Imhotep-Joseph built a massive system of storage pits—to accumulate vast amounts of grain during seven years of plenty. Later, when seven years of draught and famine strike the region, by selling its excess grain to all the starving nearby peoples, Egypt accumulates all the wealth of the entire area, becoming the most powerful nation in the mid-East." Stewart grinned as he looked around, "There is additional evidence for Egypt's wealth in a second fantastic theory by Dr. Moeller—the lavish tomb of boy-King Tutankhamen—but I'll get to King Tut later." Stewart's smile was infectious. Avi chuckled. He knew what was coming.

Stewart, continued, "For now, we're on Imhotep", he adjusted the projector.

• "It is probable that Joseph was the only person to gain Pharaoh's confidence to this degree—Joseph received every authority apart from Pharaoh himself, although he wasn't of royal blood, nor even Egyptian. And, of course, by Egyptian records, the same applies to Imhotep."

• "Dr. Moeller cites an inscription on the island of Sihiel, near the first cataract of the Nile, which actually links Imhotep to a key biblical element of the Joseph story—it tells of Pharaoh Djoser in the 18th year of his reign. The inscription states 'seven meagre years and seven rich years'. Commenting on the inscription, Moeller writes, 'Pharaoh Djoser asks Imhotep to help him with the coming seven years of famine.' All the identical biblical components of the story are there, with a similar inscription on the island of Philae in the Nile."

• "Then there is a carving in Sakkara showing starving people—their ribs prominently outlined—also depictions of sacks of grain being carried up steps in the circular silo vaults. In summary, Moeller says, 'There is no other period of famine of seven plus seven years in the history of Egypt, except for the one for which Imhotep was responsible.' In Egyptian records, only one person is described as having the administrative power to organize for Egypt's survival during a long famine—Imhotep. The similarity to biblical Joseph is precise and compelling." [185]

• "Moeller writes: 'In Egyptian text, Imhotep is called Son of Ptah, the greatest god.' and 'Joseph would be given the title of the son of Ptah, in accordance with Egyptian custom.'" [186]

• "In Egyptian records, Imhotep was chancellor to Pharaoh Djoser. In the Bible, Joseph was chancellor to an unnamed Pharaoh. In both cases there is much reference to 'second only to Pharaoh; the Bible also tells of Joseph being given Pharaoh's signet ring with the royal seal."

Stewart placed a page with many power points on the projector. "In his book Moeller cites 27 similarities in the lives, accomplishments, responsibilities and characteristics of Imhotep of Egypt and Joseph of the Bible. From the dove-tailing of their individual stories from both the Egyptian and biblical accounts, Moeller's conclusion is that the two—have to be the same person."[187]

Stewart added, "Rather than me reading these point items to you, I'll just let you skim them yourselves. 'I' is Imhotep, from Egyptian records), and, of course, 'J' is Joseph, Bible references."

I—Minister to the King of Lower Egypt.

J—"Pharaoh...made him ruler over all the land of Egypt." {Gen. 41:41-3}

I—Administrator of the Great Palace.

J—"Thou shalt be over my house." {Gen. 41:40}

I—Not of royal blood; attained position by ability.

J—From another nation and religion, not of royal blood; attained position by ability.

I—Not appointed by Pharaoh Djoser until he had reigned for some time.

J—Appointed well after Pharaoh began ruling Egypt. {Gen. 41:37-45}

I—During seven years famine, Djoser is the reigning Pharaoh (Egyptian records).

J—Joseph's Pharaoh reigns during seven years of plenty and famine. {Gen. 41:37-45}

I—Imhotep is appointed Administrator by Pharaoh Djoser during the periods of seven years famine after seven years of bountiful harvests.

J—Joseph is appointed Administrator to Pharaoh for the seven years of plenty, then of famine. {Gen. 41:37-45}

I—Ruler by "inheritance", given the status of "son" to Pharaoh.

J—Was granted the status of "son" to Pharaoh. {Gen. 41:44}

I—Was High Priest in Heliopolis.

J—Married to Asenath, daughter of Poti-Pherah, High Priest in Heliopolis, by custom, would succeed father-in-law.

I— Builder and architect (Many references).

J—Builder of grain storehouses such as at Sakkara step-pyramid, {Gen. 41:35-36}.

I—Discoverer of art of building with cut stone.

J—Storehouse at Sakkara was of cut stone.

I—Exalted by Pharaoh Djoser as of godly character.

J—"And Pharaoh said, ' a man in whom the spirit of God is.'" {Gen. 41:38}

I—Had great medical skill, he was compared to the Greek God of Healing. An inscription tells of a Greek man, healed by Imhotep from a dream.

J—Had doctors under his authority, worked by miracles, dreams, signs. {Gen: 50:2}

I—Noted as saying, "I need advice from God."

J—Noted as saying, "It is not in me; God shall give Pharaoh an answer." {Gen 41:16}

I —Decided tax rate during the seven years of famine; also not to apply to priests.

J —Decided the tax rate during the seven years of famine; also not to apply to priests. {Gen. 41:34, 47:26}

I— Realizes when he is dying. Dies at age 110.

J— Realizes when he is dying. Dies at age 110. {Gen. 50:22-24-26}

As the group was reading the list, Stewart got himself a drink, he then came back to the lectern. After awhile, he turned off the projector, getting everyone's attention.

"Our cultural world is so anti-religious," Stewart began, "that it comes as a shock to learn that there is so much solid, extra-biblical, proven data about the well-worn biblical Passover story being the cause of ancient Egypt's immense wealth and power. The seven years of famine after seven years of plenty, when excess grain was stored, came about only because Pharaoh and Joseph-Imhotep truly believed Pharaoh's dream, that seven years of famine would befall them. Today—in the 21st century, where the cultural leadership ridicules faith—I find this story astonishing." Stewart looked around. Almost everyone was nodding. He continued, "Moeller points out that Joseph/ Imhotep was primarily responsible for Egypt achieving super-wealth status, 'It was during the reign of Djoser that Egypt became a great power... great riches were accumulated during the seven years of famine...when grain was sold to all the countries around Egypt.'[182] The complex of buildings at Sakkara, has tremendous storage capacity, it is both remarkable and unique today—nothing like it has ever been seen anywhere.[183] Describing the immense storage vaults at Sakkara, Moeller writes, '40,000 cubic metres, with remnants of grain still found at the bottom.'"

Stewart, continued, "Probing into the human nature aspects of the story, it's amazing to me that Joseph-Imhotep and Pharaoh didn't just accept and squander the largesse of the good years—instead they denied themselves that bounty so as to prepare for seven lean years—only foretold in a dream. Think about it—absent a powerful faith and absolute conviction by Pharaoh that his dreams would really come to pass—I submit that normal people would have merely enjoyed and wasted the seven years of plenty!"

Truly remarkable, everyone in the group agreed: it was not only an extremely rare faith in the truth of a dream; but also the acumen and administrative ability to plan for what was needed; and then the absolute authority and the unyielding discipline to build vast granaries and store the extra grain during a prolonged period of excess.

The professor stood up to get everyone's attention. "There's a bit more in proof that Egyptian Imhotep was the biblical Joseph. Why don't you close with that?" He nodded to Stewart.

Stewart nodded back and stood up: • "Yes, it's extremely noteworthy that the mummified bodies of neither have ever been found. The known facts regarding the burials of Imhotep and Joseph also strongly support the thesis that they were the same person:

• Surrounding Imhotep's coffin in Sakkara are many clay vessels bearing the seal of Pharaoh Djoser; and the coffin is oriented to the North, not East—and it's empty; also

• Joseph would have been buried at Sakkara, his coffin orientated to the North—indicating he was not a believer in the gods of the Egyptians, who were buried facing the rising sun—East; the coffin would also be empty as Joseph's bones would have been taken by Moses with the Hebrews during the Exodus."

Everyone congratulated both Stewart and Professor Barrett about the session. The subject for the next session was selected as "Moses", Laurence to be Presenter.

(Note: Reference numbers are from "Brainwashed* and Miracles**")

Id
Circa 2000 AD, Study Group:
Hebrew Slaves in Egypt: Moses

Professor Barrett began the session with greetings, then
Laurence took over, citing historical data about Asiatic slaves
dwelling in Egypt, and about a "Moses" referred to by Egyptian
historians Eusebies and Artapanus, who lived a thousand years
after him, in the 300 BC era, "Most records," said Laurence, "are
from the library at Alexandria—that there was an Egyptian prince
Mouses, who led a military campaign against Ethiopia. There is
also much archaeological data about a slave Semitic people."
Laurence continued, using the desired power point format:

• "An Austrian dig of dwellings and tombs at Tel-ed-Daba,
Egypt, in 1989, found ancient cities near Goshen. Data from 800
drill cores gave evidence of a large number of Asian, non-
Egyptian slaves; eleven levels at the site indicate there were many
generations—during the 12th to the 13th Egyptian dynasties,
which are compatible in length and time period to the Biblical
history of the Hebrew sojourn, and as slaves in Egypt."[190]

• "There's also a 1966 Austrian archaeological research dig at Tel-ed-Daba which confirms the existence of a people with 'distinctly Israelite origins' between the 14th and 12th centuries BC, which match the period of the Hebrew Exodus and conquest of Canaan."

• "Then there's the Brooklyn Papyrus 35.1446, which tells of the reign of Pharaoh Sobekhotep; it contains over 95 names of slaves—more than half are Semitic, and seven are actual Biblical names. Really remarkable is the fact that one of the two midwives named in the Bible. 'Shiphrah', is included."[189]

• "Then there is archaeological evidence of Asiatic-type, clearly non-Egyptian, culture, including Hebrew-type houses."

• "There's also an 18th dynasty mural painting of non—Egyptian-Asian slaves having Semitic features, actually building mud-bricks from straw."

• "Also. cuneiform tablet-letters have been found in archaeological digs such as at Tel Amarna in Egypt, discoveries of the 14th to the 12th century BC. These include the well-known Pharaoh Merenptah's boast, 'Israel is laid waste', dated at 1210 BC, which confirms the presence of Israelites in lands north-east of Egypt."

• "And in direct conformity with the Bible—regarding the killing of male Hebrew babies—and the saving of baby Moses," Laurence continued, "was the discovery of unusual demographic burial data at Tel-ed-Daba—65% of the graves were of babies less than 18 months old, compared to a normal percentage of 20-30%. Appropriately also, there were far more graves of adult females than of males, which conforms to the male babies being killed at birth. Then, the story of baby Moses, floating on the Nile and saved by an Egyptian princess—Egyptian data tell of an adult Mouses." [191]

• "There is also the record of slaves building monuments—Papyrus, Leiden #348, saying, 'Distribute grain to the Habirus (Hebrews), who carry stones to the great pylon of Rameses,'" [188]

• "Regarding the military leader Mouses," said Laurence, "the Roman historian, Josephus, and a stela fragment in the British Museum, also indicate such a leader during Pharaoh Khenepres-Sobekhotep's reign. Supporting Mouses' military campaign is a statue of Sobekhotep, found on the island of Argo, establishing that Egyptian conquest and authority extended at least 200 kilometers from Egypt. Egyptian historians wrote that Mouses' fame caused Sobekhotep to target him, and forcing him (Moses) to flee to Midian—just as in the Bible story, however, the Bible and Passover Haggadah say the cause was Moses killing an Egyptian slave-driver."[192]

• Finally, said Laurence, "The Pharaoh of the Exodus is identified as King Dudimose, 36th ruler of the 13th Dynasty. In the Bible he is described as, 'Pharaoh who knew not Joseph' ".

The subject for the next session was decided on—the Ten Plagues of the Exodus, Ranah to be Presenter.

II
Circa 1300 BC, Egypt; Moses and the Ten Plagues: "The Nile is Blood" to "Death of the First-Born"

The next morning Binami awoke before dawn, dressed, donned a cloak with a golden stripe which announced to all that he was under Pharaohic protection, and made his way to the slave quarters. A guard showed him where Moses was staying. He found a seat under a tree and waited.

After a time, Moses and Aaron, leading a large crowd of Hebrews, left the compound, going toward the river Nile. Binami followed, with watchful Egyptian soldiers. At the bank of the Nile, Moses turned to the crowd, lifting his staff high with both hands, then gave it to Aaron, speaking quietly. Binami saw Aaron strike the river with it. A great cry arose, Binami watching in shock—a deep red color began swiftly spreading from the end of the staff in all directions— soon the entire Nile had become red.

"The river is blood!" cried the crowd, shrinking back in horror. Binami saw dead fish begin floating on the surface of

the water. The putrid stench of death began permeating everywhere. The Hebrews gathered closely around Moses and Aaron, as if they—the instruments of this unimaginable event—had the power to protect them.

His excitement growing, Binami saw Moses, a head taller than the throng, turn to look at a promontory where Pharaoh and his entourage were watching. Moses continued staring until, with an imperious sweep of his golden cloak, Pharaoh turned and angrily strode off.

Binami left the gathering and unobstrusively went back to the palace, seeking out Manthro. Cries of alarm and fear could be heard throughout the city, even in the palace, especially from the kitchen area where it was discovered that all water contained in pots and utensils had turned red—tasting like blood.

From the Royal chamber there was much scurrying of officials, in and out. Manthro joined the group surrounding Pharaoh. The kitchen report of water in pots turning to blood caused Pharaoh to shout in anger. Manthro suggested quietly that old wells should be examined and new wells dug to see if that source of water was also contaminated. All began clamoring for it—Pharaoh ordered it be swiftly done. Soon came reports that well water was pure and cries of relief were heard. Messengers were dispatched throughout the land to carry the good news and to encourage old wells being renewed and new ones dug.

For seven days, the Nile river was blood, and Pharaoh did not send for Moses nor did Moses seek audience with Pharaoh. During this time, Binami saw the slave girl twice. The second time he was able to brush by her fleetingly, their hands touching.

After the Nile was no longer blood, Moses and Aaron again beseeched Pharaoh to let the Israelites go, Pharaoh imperiously denying the request. Then Moses told Aaron to stretch out his hand over the Nile—and an army of frogs came out of the river to over-run Egypt. That caused Pharaoh to ask Moses to entreat his God to relent—and Moses did so and told Pharaoh that the next day the frogs would go back to the Nile—and they did. But then Pharaoh's heart hardened.

Moses then told Aaron to smite the Earth with his staff—and the dust of the earth became lice—and Pharaoh's magicians tried to do the same but could not. But Pharaoh's heart remained hardened.

Then Moses told Pharaoh, "Let my people go, or wild beasts will over-run your houses." And so it was in all of Egypt, except Goshen where dwelt the Hebrews, wild beasts over-ran all of Egypt.

Then did Pharaoh send for Moses and Aaron, "Take your people and go pray to your god—take away the beasts." And Moses appealed to God, but when the beasts were gone, Pharaoh relented of his promise and did not let the Hebrews go.

Then Moses said to Pharaoh, "Cattle in Egypt will die on the morrow, except for Goshen, if you do not let my people go." But Pharaoh's heart remained hardened, he would not let the Israelites go.

Then Moses and Aaron took soot in their hands—looking to see that Pharaoh was watching from his promontory—and threw it heavenward. Moses said, "This shall become boils and inflammation upon the skins of Egyptians." And so it did—but Pharaoh's heart remained hardened.

And Moses then said to Pharaoh, "Tomorrow there will be hail and fire and thunder, destroying cattle, even trees, if you do not let our people go." And Moses stretched forth his staff, and hail and fire and thunder descended over Egypt, destroying cattle, even trees; only in Goshen there was none.

After that plague, Pharaoh called for Moses and Aaron, "Entreat your god that there be no more." And Moses lifted his hands and the hail and thunder ceased. But Pharaoh again hardened his heart.

Then Moses and Aaron went to Pharaoh, "If you do not let us go, on the morrow will come locusts and eat everything that yet remains green in your land, even every tree." And the Egyptians cried out to Pharaoh, "Let the Israelites go." And Pharaoh asked Moses, "If I let you, who are you that will go?"

And Moses answered, "All will go, young and old, and with our flocks and herds."

But Pharaoh said, "No. Only the men can go."

So Moses stretched out his staff, and an East wind arose, carrying hordes of locusts so as to blacken the sky, and they descended upon Egypt until not a green leaf remained in all the land."

Then Pharaoh called for Moses, "I have sinned against your god—withdraw the locusts."

Therefore Moses entreated God to withdraw the locusts—and a strong West wind arose and carried all the locusts into the seas—but Pharaoh hardened his heart again and would not let the Israelites go.

Then Moses stretched out his hands to heaven—and darkness fell. For three days and nights there was absolute darkness upon the land.

Manthro called Binami to again secrete himself in the second floor drapes to see the coming meeting between Pharaoh and Moses. "The God of Moses is very powerful, each plague is worse than the one before—there is yet one more that I fear. Watch and tell me what transpires." Then he added, "Sadly, I must tell you that you are a Hebrew, and must prepare to go with them when they leave for they are your people—when whatever next happens." And he added, I know of your feelings for the slave girl, Lansel, and I will speak of her to her mistress, an old friend. We must see that she goes with you."

Without words—for he was too choked up to speak—Binami embraced the older man, the Egyptian, the closest to a father or family he had ever known.

Binami settled himself against the railing for a long wait, hidden by the curtains. The throne room was empty except for guards at the door and servants lighting the wall torches. Then voices were heard, and guards entered, surrounding Moses and Aaron. As before, they were kept a distance from the raised empty thrones. Then Pharaoh and the Royal Prince entered the chamber with their guards, and mounted their thrones.

Binami could see violent gesticulations and demanding voices as Pharaoh and Moses spoke. Then Pharaoh's words, clear and strong, "All of you may go, but your flocks must remain."

But Moses voice was firm, "Our cattle must go with us, for sacrifices to our God."

Pharaoh then said, "You will not see my face again—if you do, you will die!" Pharaoh turned and began walking.

But Moses' voice was easily heard, "You have spoken

well, Pharaoh—I will not see your face again. There will be one more plague."

When all had gone, Binami climbed down and rushed to Manthro, telling him what had transpired. Manthro was silent, thinking. Then he said, "I have arranged about the girl. At the time of the evening meal, you and she, dressed as a lad, must leave the Palace. I will accompany you as you depart. Then you must go swiftly to find her family and be with them. This night you must be within an Israelite home—I fear the God of Moses —this night will be a night of death."

Binami returned quickly to his room, gathering some clothing and belongings. He then hurried back to Manthro, who already had the girl Lansel, looking frightened, dressed as a young boy. Her face lit up when she saw Binami. They came together, their hands touching, and slowly, tears welled in both their eyes—they came closer yet—finally Binami's arms went around her and he drew her in. He could feel the quivering of her thin shoulders. He bent and briefly put his cheek to hers.

Manthro said, "We must go quickly. I will walk between you. Say nothing to anyone, even if a guard speaks to you. I will do all the talking."

Manthro in the lead, the trio walked swiftly, in the background were the sounds of the palace at the evening meal. They came to the guarded wall of the complex; Manthro spoke authoritatively to the guards and handed them some papers—there was a skeptical glance but they were waved through. Silently, Binami heaved a sigh of relief.

When they had left the palace grounds, there was but one

more guard. Binami saw Manthro give him coins. Then they were in the clear. A stones-throw further and Manthro stopped,

"This is as far as I go. You must find the girl's family and stay with them this night. With my blessings, go." Binami and Manthro embraced each other, kissing each other on the cheeks. Then Manthro turned and walked back to the palace grounds.

Binami took Lansel's hand in his as they walked quickly toward the slave section of Goshen. Darkness was falling quickly. Lansel led the way to her house, then ran ahead to greet her family. She introduced Binami to her father, a heavy-set, gruff-looking man, and her older brother Eliyah—both men were leaving to help prepare a lamb for a sacrifice and feast for that evening—as had been instructed by Moses. Her mother and sister were visiting Egyptian neighbors, Eliyah called out to them as he left.

They were soon told why. Moses and Aaron had directed all the Israelites to do several things this night: firstly to sacrifice a lamb or goat to God—to be eaten by kin families along with unleavened bread—since there would not be enough time for full baking; secondly to take along the bowls of dough for unleavened bread for the first week of traveling; thirdly to ask neighbor Egyptians for items of precious metals and jewelry—promising, somehow, that they would be responsive to such requests. Finally and most importantly, Moses told them they must daub the blood of their sacrificed animal on the doorposts and lintels of their homes—so the Angel of Death would "pass over" their house—also for all Hebrews to remain within their homes the entire night.

When Lansel's mother and sister returned, they welcomed Binami, as she had told them about him during her occasional visits home. However, everyone was busy with the evening's required activities. They were joined by two cousin families for the feast of roasted lamb; all participating in the dipping of hyssop in the lamb's blood and daubing it on the doorposts and lintels of their homes; the meal of lamb, bitter herbs and unleavened bread was perfunctory and quick, as all needed to pack belongings for the planned departure on the morrow. The meal was also very quiet, everyone speaking in hushed tones, knowing that this night would be forever memorable.

As the women cleared the table and the other families left, Lansel's brother Eliyah took Binami to an anteroom and prepared a make-shift bed for him on the floor. Gradually the house quieted as everyone retired.

At midnight, shrieks and wails began being heard from the Egyptian section, but the Hebrews remained inside their homes.

II
Circa 2000 AD, Study Group: Moses and the Ten Plagues: "The Nile is Blood" to "Death of the First-Born"!

Professor Barrett began the session with the observation that since the earliest times, to serious scholars, the ten plagues of the Exodus story had always been considered a myth, or at least a gross exaggeration, but that recent archaeological findings had thrown new light on the subject, "The Ipuwer Papyrus Scroll—Leiden 344A," he noted, "has become a highly important extra-biblical source of corroborative detail to many of the ten-plagues and Exodus events, as described in the Bible and Passover Haggadah. Found in Egypt in the early 19th century, the scroll had been taken to the Leiden Museum in Holland, where it still can be seen, and is described in both the Rohl and Moeller books. A papyrus scroll over twelve feet in length, it is called 'Admonitions of Ipuwer', written during the 19th dynasty, or the Middle Kingdom period, by a scribe/historian named Ipuwer, and interpreted in 1909 by A. H. Gardiner." The professor then nodded to Ranah, who stepped up to the lectern.

"Hi all," said Ranah. "This scroll is really remarkable—sort of makes the Haggadah Passover account seem real—describing violent events in Egypt, depicting a society in total crisis. It's like an eyewitness account of the plagues in the Exodus story. I've outlined some of the contents of the scroll in power-point format." She adjusted the focus, "I will be quoting now:"

- "'What the ancestors had foretold has happened,'—this refers to Imhotep or Joseph, who had foretold the exodus of the Hebrews from Egypt, approximately 260 years before Ipuwer." She paused;

- "This next is a key statement—the first plague, 'The river is blood...there is blood everywhere, no shortage of death... many dead are buried in the river.'"

- "'Destruction of grain,'—this could be the plague of hail or locusts."

- "'Animals moaning and roaming freely,'—this could be the fourth plague."

- "'We don't know what has happened in the land...lacking are grain, charcoal...trees are felled...food is lacking...great hunger and suffering.' This describes the eighth plague and the general chaos of a people in total panic."

- "'Darkness,'—this is clearly the ninth plague."

- "'Deaths of the children of princes, prisoners, brothers.' And this is clearly the tenth plague, the deaths of all the first-born."[194]

- "In addition to the plagues," said Ranah, "the scroll describes something unusual—the biblical description of the Israelites, just prior to the Exodus, asking their Egyptian neighbors for valuables, precious metals and jewelry: the scroll says: 'Poor...have become...of wealth...gold and lapis lazuli, silver and malachite, carnelian and bronze are strung onto the necks of female slaves'. And what the Bible says is right on, 'And they requested from the Egyptians, silver and gold articles. And God made the Egyptians favor them and they granted their requests.'" [195]

• "Also going beyond the plagues," she added, "the document corroborates the biblical description of the Exodus flight being led by a pillar of clouds by day and of fire by night: 'fire...mounted up on high ...its burning goes forth against the enemies of the land.' The Bible says: '... by night, a pillar of fire.'"[196]

"Confirming the Ipuwer Scroll," added the professor, "Bietek, in his dig at Tel-ed-Baba, which he dated to the middle of the 14th Dynasty, found shallow mass graves all over the city of Avaris— clear evidence of some type of sudden major and widespread catastrophe—not unlike what would result from a biblical 'Tenth Plague' striking all first-born. In addition, site-archaeology suggests that the remaining population had abandoned their homes quickly and en masse."[193]

There was much quiet comment about the Ipuyer Scroll versus the Bible. The subject for the following session was, "Start of the Exodus of the Hebrews from Egypt", the Presenter to be Rick.

III
Circa 1300 BC, Egypt—Exodus; Desert, Wilderness, Mountains—Trapped!

Binami was sleeping fitfully when a pounding on the door awakened him, "Get up. Get up. Moses says we must leave at mid-day!"

Binami slid himself to the floor and put on his sandals and outer garment. He had packaged the clothes he had taken from the palace into a bundle. He tied it to his waist and sat on the bed, waiting for Eliyah. Though still dark outside, one could begin to make out shapes. Together they entered the main room.

All the family was there. Binami looked for Lansel, whose eyes were on him. He smiled at her.

"Binami, did you sleep well?" Lansel's mother asked. Binami, answered politely, "Yes, thank you."

From afar they could hear shrieks and wails. Lansel's father said, "All night there have been such cries from the city. The Angel of Death must have been very busy! I heard

voices outside that Moses wants us to leave Egypt today."
He sounded uncertain, "So much to do."

Binami's years spent under Manthro's tutelage had
schooled him in organization, training him to analyze
complex concepts—he quickly grasped what was happening
to the Hebrews. After generations of slavery, of always
being told what to do and when, now they could only feel
panic, faced with uncertainty and the necessity of
immediate decisions and actions. Politely he turned to
Lansel's father, "Perhaps you and I should go out, join the
men to learn what is happening and the plans, while Eliyah
helps the women with the wagon and everything else—and
if you want to tell something to your wife, or if she has
something to tell you, both Eliyah and I will be runners, up
and back. That way, you'll both know what's going on
outside, and also with your family."

The parents looked at each other and both nodded. Then
Lansel's father said in a firm voice (which pleased Binami),
"All right, Binami and I will join the men outside, while you
all help your mother get us ready to go."

As soon as they were outside, Binami could see chaos in
the making, people running everywhere, panic on their
faces and in their voices. The two walked rapidly to where a
group had gathered, all shouting at once. The leader
seemed to be a gray-bearded man of about sixty years, who
Binami assumed was the leader of tribe Binyamin. Two
young men beside him were shouting at him. In the far
distance they could hear background wails and screams
from the Egyptian section of the city. The leader called for
the group to be quiet, then spoke up.

"We have received messages from our leader, Moses—two messengers—so nothing will be forgotten. The group quieted down, crowding around the tribal leader and the couriers—those on the outskirts shushing the people surrounding them. One of the messengers spoke, nervously but loudly:

"Moses tells us—and this is very important, everyone must take note: first—every Egyptian family has just suffered someone dying by our God and his Angel of Death, so there is much grief and fear today in every Egyptian household—even Crown Prince Tutankhamen is dead; second—in a few days, this grief will turn to great anger against us, so the Egyptian army will then follow us to attack and gain revenge; so third—today, when the sun is at mid-day, we all must begin fleeing Egypt. Moses tells us that God will be leading us so we should have no fear—we will be following a pillar of clouds by day and fire by night. But this first night we will travel throughout the darkness until the pillar of fire changes into clouds—starting with all the families who are ready and can move quickly. Moses says we must save ourselves as a people, so everyone must start sometime today; those families who are young and strong and ready to go will leave with Moses and Aaron—beginning at mid-day. The older and slower families must also hurry—as best they can—to survive."

The second messenger then spoke: "Moses says we must organize and avoid panic: first, we will travel as tribal groups and within each tribe as family units. Each family should agree to always be with one or two other families, of kin or friends as a basic core unit, all remaining together and helping each other, so no family is ever alone; second, in addition to the family units, all young men, from eighteen to *thirty who are not needed for their personal families, will become part of a military group under Joshua, and will be trained as scouts and warriors; third, each leader, like tribal leaders and Joshua, is to pick an assistant, a second-in-command—they will exchange positions every other day, so one will always be with Moses, the other with his tribe. Each will have two messenger-runners always with them, picked from their own tribes, who will exchange information with the leaders, passing-up to Moses any problems and passing down all orders; fourth, Moses will pick someone to be leader of a special group of skilled workmen to repair wagons and equipment, everything that will be needed for a long, hard trip. This leader also will have an aide and two messengers; also Miriam, Moses' sister, will head a group of women who will see to food and care for the sick and elderly—she also will have an assistant with two messengers."*

The messenger paused to catch his breath, then continued, "Lastly—and Moses says this is most important—the family groups under the tribal leaders— they must appoint leaders of three core family units, six to nine families, with an assistant and one messenger each; then a leader of a group of five such groups, each with an assistant and one messenger; and for each grouping of five family groups, another higher order group leader and assistant, each with a messenger. So says our leader Moses—this is what we must do to escape from Egypt as a unified people, the Bnai Israel. Those families that are ready to travel must begin at mid-day and continue all night—and Joshua will pick scout-fighters to travel ahead of the families, on both sides and behind. So orders our leader Moses."

When he was done, the first messenger, added: "Aaron also tells us we must pray before we depart—as you and your families leave your homes, and also each morning and night, you must all say to yourselves—and with all your children, 'The God of Moses and Bnai Israel has protected me from death and will protect me and my family from the Egyptians—and will lead us to a promised land.'"

Binami's thoughts as he heard the detailed instructions from Moses were that Manthro would have greatly approved such organized planning. The leader of Tribe Binyamin then appointed someone to be his second-in-command and then instructed everyone to return to their homes, to prepare to leave as soon as they were able. He also said that the heads of all households that would not be ready to depart at mid-day were to notify him.

When Binami and Lansel's father returned to their house, they found that Eliyah and the women were well along in packing. They had denied themselves the taking of too much of household belongings or clothing, only what could be carried on their wagon. They had one cow, which they had tied to the wagon. Lansel's mother had put the remaining food, fruit and unleavened bread on the table. "Come, eat quickly, our last meal at home—where we and our families have lived all our lives."

It had been 430 years to the day that the Israelites had dwelt in Egypt, since the time of Joseph—whose bones, Moses was taking with him.

The three cousin families that had together eaten the sacrificed lamb, decided to team together—all began moving toward the open field. Then, at mid-day, a tall pillar of white cloud suddenly appeared where Moses and Aaron were standing. Shouts and gasps could be heard from the assemblage of Israelites. Binami felt his heart pound. He moved toward Lansel and grasped her hand, drawing her alongside, so that her elbow was inside his. He felt tears welling up and saw she was weeping openly—he noticed her parents and many of the Hebrews were also. With a gruff command from her father, they all took the first step forward.

It was a long procession, three or four families abreast, wagons and cattle with children running about excitedly. As they found a place in the convoy, everyone gradually became strangely quiet, until there was only the creaking of wagons and the lowing of cattle that could be heard. It was as if everyone was thinking of the uncertainty and dangers that lay ahead. Even though they had been slaves, their lives and burdens had been organized, predictable, even tolerable, if barely so. Now no-one knew what the future held.

Far ahead of them was the pillar of clouds. In the days and weeks to come, it would become a beacon for hope and faith, proof that a power, far greater than even Pharaoh's, was leading them—to a promised "land of milk and honey".

A strong-looking man riding in an Egyptian one-horse chariot, came up—looking the family over. He singled out Binami and Eliyah, "I am Joshua, I want you two for scout-fighters. Report to Chanay, my number two, up ahead." Then he sped off.

The pace of travel gradually settled into a slow, steady march, so the family seemed able to push and pull the wagon without the two young men. With shrugs and slightly prideful smiles, Eliyah and Binami said good-bye and began loping on ahead to find Chanay.

As strong, athletic young men, fast runners, they were soon absorbed into Joshua's new army of scouts and warriors. Binami, as a palace Prince, had had military training of spear-throwing and combat with sword and shield, so was soon selected by Joshua to be an instructor to the raw recruits, as well as a potential team leader.

Since Binami's military experience also included chariots and horses, he and Joshua's second, Chanay, were sent by Joshua to scout—on the very first evening—to see what the Egyptian army was doing. Going far past the tail-end of Israelite straggler-families, back to the Egyptian army camp, they hid behind a small clump of trees, away from the camp's outer edge. Settling down for a long wait, they ate unleavened bread they had taken along, then took turns listening to the camp noises, then slept on the ground. As dawn broke, Chanay carefully crept forward, searching the camp for suspicious movement, while Binami kept the horse quiet and the chariot ready for a quick departure. No-one was to be seen, although wails of grief could still be heard in the distance.

After the sun had risen to mid-morning, Chanay, crouching low, came back, and they took off in the chariot, walking the horse at first to minimize noise. After they had covered some distance and felt safe, they put the horse at full gallop, then after a satisfying amount of time and significant distance traveled, first Chanay and then Binami got out to run beside the slowly trotting and resting horse. Young and strong runners, they were soon passing straggling Hebrew family groups. As they approached Lansel's family, Binami *jumped from the chariot, and with a shout of unabashed joy, grabbed and hugged her, ignoring her father's frown. He then ran alongside the chariot and Chanay to find Joshua.*

Binami stood quietly beside Chanay as he reported what they had seen—that there seemed to be no organized assemblage of soldiers, horses or chariots. Joshua nodded, but added, "Not as yet." He then grunted approval of Binami, dismissing him for the day. He then took Chanay to report to Moses.

It became a pattern, every other day, Chanay and Binami would go past the tail-end of Hebrew families in the fast-moving chariot, looking for any indication of Egyptian military activity. On alternate days, Binami and Eliyah on foot, scouted ahead and on the sides of the Hebrews. Despite the concern for the dangers they faced, Binami found himself full of joy, as day followed day with no evidence of Egyptian pursuit. The routine was monotonous, but for him and Lansel, there had been an awakening of happiness in each other, even an excitement in their anticipation of the next quick embrace and kiss—as he left each morning and his return each evening—when they could snuggle in each others arms and talk of a future life together.

The pillar of clouds—after the first day and night of prolonged travel—had remained stationary for a full day, as if knowing that a respite was needed by this people, so unused and unprepared for such an arduous flight, previously knowing only slavery in Egypt. Many families had taken too much in clothing, belongings and household goods; some wagons were unequal to the demand of rough terrain and had broken down, thus the wake of the Hebrew Exodus for the first few days was strewn with many and varied discards. It would take some time to adjust and readjust, to condition the many thousands of slave people to the daily grind of plodding, hour after hour into unfamiliar territory. But days passed into weeks, and gradually the Israelites settled into the routine, a steady pace of pushing and pulling the wagons, going around hills and valleys, steadily putting distance behind themselves and from Egypt. However, the scouts had begun reporting—for a week now—that Egyptian chariots were trailing them. To protect the slowest Hebrew families, Moses and Joshua had immediately assigned thirty scout-warriors stationed permanently behind to protect and help the slowest Hebrews, Joshua and Chanay alternating positions every other day. And every day, Joshua held combat practice for his men.

The problems of wagons and the old and weak had gradually been resolved by the harsh necessity of speed, plus Moses' organizational system. Joshua informed his scout-warrior group that Moses had said they were traveling the same route he had taken forty years before, when he had fled to Midian—but led now by God and his pillars of cloud and fire.

Then a new problem arose—predator bands of Amelekites, Bedouin nomads of the desert, murderers and thieves who preyed upon the weakest and most helpless stragglers of the Hebrews, swiftly attacking, killing, plundering. Under increasing threat as the Israelites went deeper into the wilderness, two-thirds of Joshua's army was *now assigned to protect the Hebrews—they soon became skilled combat veterans and victors.*

Finally, they reached a large body of water, called Yam Suf by Moses. But then, as they neared the tip, while Moses had previously circled north of it, abruptly the pillar of clouds turned south, moving along its western shore. When that happened, Binami saw that Joshua had become worried. The terrain also, was now becoming hilly, with mountains seen in the distance. Joshua's alarm grew as the land became more and more rugged, especially as the pillar of clouds, after two days, turned eastward, now leading the Hebrews—strung out in a single family convoy—along a narrow and twisting wadi, a dried river bed. The forward scouts then reported that the wadi ended into an open, extremely large, flat, sandy beach—on the shore of Yam Suf—and Yam Suf was a very long, very wide and deep sea. Clearly alarmed, Joshua, took Chanay, Binami and several of his top scouts with him, and sought out Moses and Aaron at the head of the procession of families. All but the trailing families were now well into the narrow, winding and dangerous wadi.

"We are being entrapped," Joshua said to Moses and Aaron. "The pillar of clouds is taking us along a winding, narrow wadi, and to a large flat and open beach—with impassable mountains on both sides and the deep Yam Suf in front. There is no place where we can hide or escape. The Egyptian army is behind us and coming closer each day. We will be slaughtered in the wadi or on the open beach!" He took a deep breath, then continued, "Yam Suf is long and deep—our scouts can barely see across it. We have no ships and there are no trees to build rafts. We cannot wade or swim

across. When Pharaoh overtakes us we will surely be trapped and helpless!"

Binami held his breath, watching as Moses and Aaron listened to Joshua in silence. Moses then put his hands on Joshua's shoulders, and said, "Our God has shown us his power. What you have said, Joshua, is true, as also is what our eyes can see and our minds can imagine. But we must put our faith in our Lord."

Binami, his heart pounding, watched as Moses turned, followed by Aaron, and they continued walking forward, following the pillar of clouds as it moved ahead.

At the end of the wadi Binami could now see the long, wide beach and the dark waters of Yam Suf—and the pillar of clouds slowly moving across the beach and toward the water.

Joshua, still worried, sent his group of scouts to join their families. Gradually, as the Israelites left the wadi, they began gathering on the beach. By late afternoon almost the entire Hebrew people, with their flocks of animals and wagons had assembled on the gigantic beach.

It was then that Binami noticed that the pillar of clouds had disappeared from in front; a gasp went up from the multitude. Sounds of fear, of moanings and wailings could be heard everywhere as night-time approached and there was no pillar of fire to inspire confidence. Mutterings were heard from all sides, "Better that we should be slaves in Egypt—rather than die here in the wilderness."

III
Circa 2000 AD, Study Group: Exodus: Desert, Wilderness, Mountains—Trapped!

"It is truly amazing", said Professor Barrett, opening up the next session, "how biblical scholars, even learned Rabbis, have been taken in by the conventional wisdom about the Exodus— whether there is any truth or not to the story: the escape of a slave people: the miraculous crossing of a Yam Suf, the Red Sea, and its location; or if there really was then, or is still, a Mount Sinai? Were the many descriptions of the surroundings of Mount Sinai exaggerated? One sees advertisements about a tour trip to Mount Sinai, and pilgrims, or adventurers, or curiosity-seekers, who are then taken to a monastery in the lower Sinai peninsula—where there's nary a single topographical landmark that is consistent with biblical description of Mount Sinai, Yet, that's the centerpiece for the Ten Commandments, the basis for the moral code of our Judean-Christian civilization, and the philosophy of human-kind for two millennia. How can that be?"

"Yes," chimed in Rick, "but we must remember sixteen centuries of dominating thought—" "Propaganda—" interrupted Stewart, "—establishes a very powerful belief system."

"Not being religious,—" said the newest participant to the group, a no-nonsense feminist lawyer, Serah, "—what do you mean, sixteen centuries?"

"Well", explained Rick, "Constantine, in the fourth century AD, adopted monotheism and Christianity, taking with him the Roman Empire at first, then the entire civilized world. The influence on him was his mother. On a trip to the mid-East, she claimed to have a vision that the biblical Mount Sinai was a nearby mountain in lower Sinai—either Mount Jabal Katerina, now marked by St. Catherine's monastery, or Jabal Al Musa, Mountain of Moses, built about 350 AD, monks having lived there ever since[235]. That's where the world accepts the biblical Mount Sinai as being located, in lower Sinai Peninsula—tour trips take pilgrims to one or the other—neither having a match with any biblical features of Mt. Sinai: like the piles of stones around it, or altars, or pillars—and no one seems to care, because religion is not believed in by our cultural elite."

"OK," asked Serah, "But why do you say 'even scholars' have been taken in?"

"Well," said Rick, "If Mount Sinai is in the Sinai Peninsula, then the crossing of Yam Suf would have to have taken place closer to Egypt, thus the crossing site had to be either the Bitter Lakes or the tip of the Gulf of Suez. But those bodies of water are shallow, raising a plausibility question of the drownings of Egyptians with their chariots and horses."

Lawrence interrupted, "There's also the curiously overlooked fact that, elsewhere in the Bible, the same phrase 'Yam Suf' clearly refers to the right arm of the historical Red Sea—the Gulf of Aqaba. Thus, in 1 Kings 9:26, 'King Solomon built a fleet of ships at Etzion Geber near Elath on the shore of Yam Suf, in the land of Edom.' The city at its northern tip is still called Eilat. Interestingly—" he added, displaying a bit of research knowledge, "—scholars have suggested that the name 'Red Sea' is probably due to the reddish tint reflected from the neighboring mountains.'"[236]

Ranah added, "Ancient maps also show that the land of Midian —where young Moses fled, later finding himself on Mount Horeb —another name for Mt. Sinai —is not in the Sinai Peninsula at all, but is 'east' of the Gulf of Aqaba. Also ignored are over a hundred biblical references which state that Moses and the Hebrews 'came out from the land of Egypt' —and the Sinai Peninsula has always been 'in' Egypt, part of it, not 'out' of it—all this evidence has been dismissed by scholars, even Hebrews, for centuries!" [241]

"So, where did all this recent knowledge come from?" asked Serah.

Rick said, "Initially, it was really recent 'Indiana-Jones' type adventurers, apparently religious Christian mountain climbers, who searched out Jabal Al Laws, the highest mountain in northwest Saudi Arabia. With derring-do, they crawled under a Saudi barbed-wire fence and climbed the mountain, about 7000 feet high —taking pictures, although forbidden, and making notes and sketches. What they found—and it's confirmed by photos in a half-dozen books and an expeditionary diving film — all available on the Internet —was that the features of Jabal Al Laws and surrounding topography, apparently meet all the biblical descriptions of Mount Sinai.". He opened up a notebook:

"Firstly, the location conforms to Biblical geography that Midian, where young Moses fled Egypt, was not in the Sinai Peninsula but was 'east' of the Gulf of Aqaba."[240]

Lawrence interrupted, "The earliest placement of Mt. Sinai in lower Sinai Peninsula was probably when the Hebrew Bible was first translated into Greek, circa 250 BC. Hebrew scholars really ignored their own Torah for centuries. Ancient documents placed Mount Horeb or Mt. Sinai—in the land of Midian, which is now Saudi Arabia—not in the Sinai Peninsula. Yet all this was ignored."

"The power of universal propaganda," said Stewart, "they even renamed Yam Suf—which used to mean 'Red Sea', into 'Sea of Reeds'—that's the translation even found today in almost every English-language Bible in America, even those in orthodox synagogues."

Rick found Serah's newly-found interest to be stimulating: "After the adventurers opened it up, there were several teams and expeditions of religious Christians—and really, all of this is only in recent years. They did their proper homework as to biblical locations, then began mountain-climbing and sea-diving— exploring in Saudi Arabia and finding the real Mount Sinai—after that, they found the provably-true Red Sea crossing site—an underwater ridge spanning the entire width of the Gulf of Aqaba, about seven miles in length."

"How can you mean, 'provably-true'" asked Serah, her growing interest evident in her tone. The others all tried to answer at once, but Rick persevered. "Just only years ago, in 2000, amazing discoveries were made by a diving expedition in the Gulf of Aqaba, using both deep sea divers and an underwater submersible with cameras. Astonishingly, coral-covered chariot wheel artifacts from ancient Egypt were photographed on that undersea ridge in the Gulf of Aqaba—and there were many highly-credentialed, world-renowned scientists, archaeologists and historians on the expedition, providing scholarly oversight and also testifying to the credibility of the findings." [255]

"Isn't that amazing," said Bethe, unable to contain her excitement, "—and these incredible discoveries really raise a 21st century consideration of the biblical miracle of the splitting of the sea—how can it be ignored? After all, how explain coral-covered wheels of 13th Dynasty Egyptian chariots, wreckage strewn along the under-sea ridge path, going from Egypt to Saudi Arabia—along with bones of men and horses—all exactly as described in the Bible?" Bethe paused for emphasis, "All of which supports the drowning of the Egyptian chariot army, even including Pharaoh —which brings us, face to face, with the question of 'Why are those Egyptian chariot wheels there?'—leading into—by hard logic—a seeming 'miracle' of the splitting of the sea."

Rick, nodding to Bethe, continued, "There was also the discovery of the true Mount Sinai—in Saudi Arabia, and with all the topographical attributes as described in the Bible. These include altars, with drawings on them of the uniquely-shaped horns of Aphis bulls —certainly out-of-place in the Arabian desert, hundreds of miles from Egypt."

"Not to mention the amazing discovery of Rephidm" said the professor, "Imagine, two sixty-foot solid rock shafts—with an absolutely parallel, twenty-inch gap between them—where Moses, per the Bible, struck a rock in anger, twice, and split it—to get water. It is a startling sight, available on the Internet—a gigantic, five-story-high perfectly split rock. One immediately concludes it's either solid proof that the Bible story is true, or these colossal rock shafts were crafted in Hollywood studios."

"Wow," said Serah, "Can this really be true—with apparently so few people knowing about any of this—including me? I've got to research this out myself."

"Wait a second", said Avi, "You're putting the cart—or, I should say 'chariot'—before the horse—what precedes all that, and also explains a mysterious phrase in written history—what the Bible says Pharaoh said—and what comes from modern satellite photography of the area. If you 'Google' Wadi Watir and Nuweiba Beach of the Gulf of Aqaba, you'll see a 'right-on' depiction of the words in the Bible attributed to Pharaoh—'the Israelites are entangled—or trapped—in the wilderness'—the satellite pictures show it to be exactly that. The wadi dry river wanders between impassable rugged hills, then ends at a huge flat, open and sandy beach, maybe a mile on a side—and that's where the Israelites were —apparently trapped: behind them was the Egyptian army; they were strung out along a narrow, meandering wadi in rugged, rocky terrain; in front of them was a flat open, sandy beach, and then the daunting Gulf of Aqaba."

"Interesting also," added Bethe, "Roman-Jewish historian Josephus, given the temple scroll records for his research because he helped Rome in their destruction of Jerusalem and Solomon's Temple, uses the exact same expression to denote the helplessness of the Hebrews—'they are trapped in the wilderness.'"

Rick summarized for Serah, "The Israelites had no place to hide or escape—Pharaoh and his chariots were behind them, impassably hilly ground was on both sides, and ahead was a deep sea.

The subject for the next session was "The Crossing of Yam Suf and Egyptian Chariots", Serah indicating she wanted to research the subject and be the Presenter.

IV
Circa 1300 BC, Exodus:
Yam Suf; Walls of Water;
Egyptian Chariots

It had been a night of fear for the Hebrew people, encamped on the immense beach, huddling together to keep warm and to allay personal fears. Behind them, in the distance, they could see the glow of the Egyptian campfires in the wadi and surrounding hills—and hear their taunting cries. Joshua had moved his army of scout-warriors— except for Chanay and Binami, who he charged with attending Moses and Aaron—to protect the entrance to the beach, taking up defensive positions between the Hebrews and the Egyptians. Binami and Eliyah, as they left Lansel and her family, whispered for them to be brave, that Moses was very confident that their God would protect them.

As dawn lightened the eastern sky, Binami saw Moses and Aaron standing silently at the edge of the water. Moses turned to the group of tribal leaders and said, "This day will our Lord gain honor for freeing Bnai Israel—Pharaoh and the Egyptian chariot army will be seen no more." Then he turned to face the water, lifting his arms and staff to the heavens.

A strong East wind arose as if by magic. Binami, could see far out in the distance what appeared to be a small line in the water—as he watched, it grew rapidly until he could see what it was—the sea seemed to be splitting, water moving away from the center to both sides, which were becoming walls of roiling water. The parallel lines grew steadily larger, and Binami could see that a trough was being created as the waters were swept to either side— becoming the churning walls. As the phenomenon drew ever closer, Binami could see that the bottom of the trough was a sandy pathway. As he watched in amazement, this splitting of the sea drew ever closer, until it reached the feet of Moses, standing at the edge of the immense beach. Binami, near Moses, could see even at the edge, where beach became pathway, the water, although only a finger thickness in depth, was still being swept to the sides of the pathway—a tiny rill of water-wall on both sides.

It was an incredible sight. Everyone close, seeing it, seemed numb with amazement—then there were shouts of joy, and "Bless the Lord, our God", could be heard from the tribal leaders and everyone nearby. The joyous exclamations became an explosion of sound as thousands of Israelites shouted their relief and delight at the miracle, and its portent for saving them.

"Go," cried Moses. "Enter, Bnai Israel, see what our Lord has done for us. Go and be saved!"

Binami surveyed the mass of Hebrews, but saw no-one move, then Moses pointed his staff at a short, burly, black-

bearded man in his middle years: "Nachman, you —you are a leader, your faith is strong. Show these Israelites! Lead the way!"

With a shout, Nachman, holding a child in his arms, began pushing through the crowd, which opened up before him. His wife and a small daughter were behind him, trailing them, a young man pulling, and a young woman pushing their wagon. Nachman went a stone's throw along the descending path, his family following. When his eyes reached the water level at the sides of the path-way—the water held back, seemingly, by the wind—he moved to a side of the path, staring at the wall of water, which churned, but magically, did not flow over onto the sunken sand-path on which he and his family were standing.

Binami, his heart pounding with excitement, then saw Nachman turn and wave, then his wife and children, calling out for the Israelites to join them. Only a few at the edge of the path moved forward—then all began crowding in a surge. Many, when the water was well over the level of their heads, looked wonderingly at the side-walls of water, but continued to move resolutely along the path. With shouts of joy, the assembled mass of Hebrews was now pressing forward to follow the leaders.

Moses then ordered Chanay to send Binami to tell Joshua what had happened—then he, Aaron, Chanay and the tribal leaders, took their first steps onto the descending, now dry, pathway.

Binami pushed his way through the excited crowd of Hebrew families and wagons, shouting about the miracle of the walls of water being held back by God, which would give them a pathway to cross the sea to safety. He stopped to embrace Lansel, retelling again the miracle he had witnessed.

Joshua could hardly believe what Binami told him; he had heard the shouts of the Israelites and was beginning to see forward movement in the packed crowd, pressing to escape from the beach where they felt trapped and vulnerable.

"How long do you think before all the families will be off this open beach", asked Binami. Joshua pursed his lips, "Most of the day", he said. "for all to get to the seashore and begin moving down the pathway, hopefully, to safety."

Binami saw that Joshua had divided his forces in two, sending half to help the Israelite families, the other half to remain behind as a barrier against the Egyptian army. Joshua's latter group was spread out at arms-length-distance apart, to cover as much of the broad width of the beach-front as possible—kneeling in alert defensive positions. Then, when the group of scout-warriors traveling with the Hebrew-stragglers had covered a bow-shot distance, at a shout they would turn, kneel in defensive readiness, holding such position while the first soldier group would run up to them and past—in turn, to be protective of the tail-end families. In this stop-and-run manner, Joshua's men were helping both lagging Hebrew families and being defensive against the Egyptians.

The wide curtain of cloud which had befogged the end of the wadi, meanwhile, had begun traveling forward onto the beach, in step with Joshua's men. In this manner both Israelites and the curtain of clouds were advancing in staccato fashion across the huge sandy beach and toward the water's edge. At mid-day they had made considerable progress, and Joshua sent Binami to report back to Moses.

Binami sped along at a long-stride lope, covering ground quickly, When passing Lansel's family, he was happy to see *that they had now entered upon the pathway. He noted the increasing angle of the descending slope, which made the first part easy to traverse, but would bode difficulty for the final ascending portion. He sped on, passing nervous but jubilant Hebrews. He experienced the queer feeling in the pit of his stomach of seeing the walls of water rising high above his head on both sides of the path-way.*

After awhile, the path had become flat, then it began climbing, and now everyone was required to push and pull the wagons. Binami helped a few struggling families, but pressed on. Finally, he could see the opposite shore, a narrow strip of beach, then Moses, taller than everyone else, close to the shore-line. Finally he fell in behind Moses, the shore only a stone's throw away. Binami waited respectfully, until Moses had gained the beach and had turned to face him.

Moses was silent as Binami made his report of the positions of Joshua's forces, the Egyptians, and the last of the Israelites—as of an hour or so earlier. Moses asked if he was tired and wanted someone else to report back to Joshua, but Binami shook his head—he was too excited to do anything else but return. He only needed a refreshing drink of water and a short rest.

The return was difficult as Binami was interweaving his way against the flow of Israelite families, wagons and cattle. When he finally reached the beginning of the pathway and the gigantic beach, the sun was passing over the horizon, dusk would soon fall—Binami was happy to see that almost all the Israelites were now on the pathway. He met Joshua at the beach edge and told him the status.

Joshua nodded, "Good work Binami. you can now rest for awhile. My forces will be here shortly, and together we will begin the crossing."

Gratefully, Binami sank down onto the still-warm sand. As he looked far across the expanse of the beach seeking the Egyptians, he saw that the front edge of the fog curtain had now moved well onto the beach—though still very far away, he could make out small figures of horses and chariots through the mist at the edge of the wadi. The cloud cover was serving its purpose well. All the Israelites would be halfway across the sea and safety by the time the first Egyptian chariots would reach the edge of the beach and the start of the pathway.

More tired than he had thought, Binami had fallen into a light sleep when Joshua wakened him—a partial moon was now arising, and the scout-warriors were leaving the beach-front and stepping onto the pathway. Binami, now refreshed, although his muscles were still tired, jumped up and joined Joshua and his men. They began an easy athlete's trot, taking advantage of the downward slope, the pathway being readily visible in the moonlight. However, the dim light prevented seeing whether the Egyptians had now gained the beach; but even if so, they were still too far away to be heard. Confident now, Joshua's army progressed steadily but silently.

Soon they reached the point where the pathway became level, almost halfway, then where it began to rise—then the trailing scout began shouting that he could hear sounds of the Egyptians in the distance, that they had probably reached the pathway. The Hebrews quickened their pace, knowing that the Egyptians pursuing in horse-drawn chariots were much faster. There was enough moonlight for the determined Hebrews to press on. Faint trumpet sounds and shouts of the Egyptians were now heard by all.

His heart pounding, Binami forced his tired muscles not to slow down. The pathway was now at a significant upward slope. Finally they could see and hear Moses, Aaron and the Israelites on the shore, urging them onward. Grimly they held their pace. Now there were the sounds of chariots, the snorting of horses and Egyptian voices coming ever closer. The shore line, visible now as pre-dawn light streaked the sky, was only a bowshot away, the first Egyptian chariot not much further behind the last Hebrew. An outstretched arm finally grabbed Joshua then Binami, pulling them onto the strip of sandy shore. Finally the last of Joshua's men reached shore—and an arrow from the first chariot struck him in the leg.

Moses, his brow furled, stood at the shoreline staring at the onrushing chariot. He held up his staff, pointing it over the pathway and then to the walls of water. Binami held his breath, the Israelites quieted, hypnotized by fear. Then there was a rush of sound—an unfamiliar sound, as of muffled thunder—and Binami saw that the nearby walls of water had begun to collapse.

The first Egyptian chariot was a stone's throw away when the tumbling water from the falling walls swept up the chariot and horse, overturning them, both charioteer and horse floundering in the turbulence, the water about two-man's-height in depth. Finally, Binami saw the chariot sink below the surface, followed by the Egyptian, wearing heavy armor, his arms flailing.

Dumb-founded, Binami watched the lines of collapsing walls of water, now speeding swiftly backwards along the pathway; then finally the sea—as far as he could see in the dawn's first light—was becoming normal, smooth and calm, with soft undulating surface waves.

A hundred thousand voices filled the air with shouts of joy.

IVa
Circa 2000 AD, Study Group: Exodus: Hypothetical—A Topological "Set-up" Since Time Began!

As the next session began, Serah could hardly contain her enthusiasm, "I've really researched these chariot wheels and Mount Sinai—it's incredible that the whole world is seemingly unaware of all this—including me until last month. But now I've read four or five books such as 'Mountain of Moses', 'The Gold of Exodus', 'The Exodus Case', and so on; and I've seen the documentary film 'The Exodus Revealed'. Absolutely remarkable—and Dr. Moeller's book with all those artifacts about Joseph being Imhotep—then there's King Tut's tomb, that the world apparently knows nothing about. It's really exciting—iconoclastic!"

Professor Barrett held up his hand, "Let's slow down. What we want is hard evidence proving the Exodus story happened; we were at the point where the Israelites were about to start their flight from Egypt. Now, what do we have of extra-biblical data to pick up from there?" He looked around the group— "OK, let's hear from Serah."

Serah cleared her throat and stood up, smiling. "I've been listening to all you knowledgeable people for many months, but these past weeks I've learned much and thought about it much— and I would like to, perhaps, shock you all—with a 'hypothetical',", Serah paused for emphasis, "What we have is quite remarkable—21st century data, knowledge and logic to argue a most incredible case—especially from an atheist and skeptic, like me. My hypothetical—from solid artifacts and topography—is that there is, or was, a 'Creator', and that this entity set up a topological 'prop', eons ago, for what appears to be a miraculous land-sea situation in regard to the Exodus of a Semitic slave people from Egypt, and the drowning of their pursuers."

The Red Sea Crossing Site   Gulf of Aqaba – Undersea Path

Nuweiba Beach   Section Across Gulf of Aqaba

Slope 1:20   Undersea Path   Slope 1:14

Basic Sea Floor, Eilat Deep

Section Along Center of Gulf of Aqaba

Eilat Deep (3000 ft.)   Aragonese Deep (5000 ft.)

Presentation by Serah to University Study Group (Hypothetical Argument)

There were smiles and chuckles from the group, open laughter from Lawrence. Serah smiled self-consciously and continued, "Yes, I know, I know—but, here's the deal—I'm two things that make me perfect for just such a topic and approach—first, I'm at least an agnostic, a non-believer; and second, I'm a trial lawyer— and during this past week, after absorbing what we've learned about the unusual topography: that narrow, meandering dry wadi, that giant beach, and especially that long, undersea pathway with a deep sea on both sides! What I found myself doing, lying in bed at night, was quite unusual—I began laying out the case —as if I had a legal-client who was a true believer—the case basis being that all this extremely unusual topography looks like a prop 'set-up', planned from the beginning of time. The unusual features of wadi and an incredible volume of sand to build up the undersea ridge-path from the sea floor—thousands of feet below water level—establishes a unique physical situation." She paused, and with a smile, looked around. "Firstly, the Hebrews, stretched out along the wadi, chased by Egyptian chariots, become truly trapped, blocked on all sides; then secondly, the 'set-up' of the 'sea-level' ridge path which becomes the means of their escape; thirdly, that it then becomes the death-trap of the pursuing chariot army! Wow! All it would take would be a small, timely Earthquake or tremor to shake down that three-thousand-foot-high, built-up ridge-path to its present undersea level—or a miraculously, concentrated East wind to split the sea!" Serah laughed. "Now, how about that? Do you want to hear it in more detail?" "Of course", all said almost together, the professor adding, "Go ahead, this should be good."

Serah took some notes from a briefcase, put them on the lectern—then began pacing, like an attorney before final argument. She seemed to lose herself in her presentation. "The topography at the Gulf of Aqaba, eastern appendage of the Red Sea, is so unusual as to beg two questions. First, if there was and is a God—wanting to show humankind 'miracles', such as: a) the splitting of a long, deep sea, walls of water being held back—somehow, perhaps by an East wind; b) to reveal an undersea pathway which leads to safety in another land, seven miles away; c) which could thus be used for the escape of a slave-people chased by a chariot army; and d), but then becomes the means of engulfing and drowning the pursuing chariots;" She looked around, "or, the second question—not even needing a sea-splitting miracle—the build-up of a ridge-way path, thousands of feet above the sea floor—seven miles of length—then, at an opportune moment, the Egyptian chariots strung along it, a minor Earth tremor shakes the ridge—"

Serah looked around the group. "Doesn't that require the precise, amazing and completely improbable set-up that we—as 21st century realists and skeptics—can easily verify, by a trip to the Mid-East or even while at home on the Internet? What are the solid, scientific facts?

"1. During this recent decade, photos viewable in a dozen books plus underwater film—show coral-covered wreckage of 15th to 18th Dynasty Egyptian Chariot wheels of 3500 years ago, strewn along an undersea ridge-path which bridges the Gulf of Aqaba from Nuweiba Beach on the Sinai Peninsula, to Saudi Arabia."

"2. The Gulf of Aqaba, about 100 miles long and seven or eight miles wide, connects with the Red Sea at the Straits of Teran; it is extremely deep, 5000 feet, the Argonese Deep, on one side of an undersea ridge-path, and 3000 feet, the Eilat Deep, on the other side. The depth of the sea has been well probed and verified."

"3. Satellite photos show a stretched-out, winding wadi, or dried river bed, leading to Nuweiba Beach, a large sandy expanse, about a mile on a side, extending into the Gulf—where the undersea ridge pathway begins."

"4. The undersea pathway is described by Dr. Lennart Moeller—medical research scientist, marine biologist and archaeologist, the leader of a diving expedition there a decade ago—as being strewn with coral-covered chariot wheels, axles and shafts, even some skeletal bones of horses and men. Dr. Viveka Ponten, archaeologist and deep-sea diver, who had also been doing similar diving-research for years off the shore of Saudi Arabia, corroborates the findings in her book. On the expedition were a half-dozen world-class scientists from three continents, providing both scholarly oversight and testifying to the truth of the discoveries: Dr. Frank Moore Cross, world-renowned Archaeologist and Professor Emeritus of Harvard University; Dr. John A. Bloom, Director of the Interdisciplinary Biblical Research Institute; Dr. Bryant C. Wood, Director of Association for Biblical Research; Dr. C. S. Lewis; et al. Diving photographs were taken by a remote-controlled undersea craft with camera, plus divers, including both Drs. Moeller and Ponten."

"5. Per marine biology, coral does not grow on rocks and sand, only on man-made wooden or metallic objects, retaining the initial shape of the underlying structure. There is no other spot on earth, even in the same Gulf of Aqaba, which contains such coral-covered chariot wreckage. The wheel diameters and number of spokes, six and eight, match the chariots found in King Tut's tomb and are as shown on Egyptian wall murals of that dynastic period."

"6. The entry area to Nuweiba Beach is that dry river bed— Wadi Watir, shown on satellite photography as twisting and turning between rugged hills. The undersea ridge begins at the beach's projection into the Gulf, obviously created by sand-silt deposits over millennia—which then continued to deposit such a volume of sand as to almost completely fill the Gulf, nearly a mile deep and seven miles wide."

"7. For most of the distance to Saudi Arabia, the ridge-path is several hundred feet below sea level. The slopes of the ridge are twelve and fourteen degrees, which are traversable inclinations, at both the Sinai and Saudi Arabia ends."

"8. During 3500 years, undoubtedly turbulent storms have swept much chariot-wreckage over the sides of the ridge down to the sea floor, thousands of feet below—however, enough artifacts remain to prove the happenings of millennia ago."

"9. To a realist—large volumes of sand are not unusual—on ocean coastline beaches. However, such an immense volume of sand as to create a mile-size beach and to nearly fill the almost mile-deep gorge across seven miles—all from the sand-silt runoff of an average-looking river wadi—has to be so unusual that it beggars the mind. Yet, there it is, on the Internet—enabling the playing-out of the Biblical scene: Hebrews somehow escaping on foot across a wide, very deep sea, and later, a chariot army being drowned. That's what both topography and artifacts show."

"10. And there is, of course, solid before-and-after verification of the Exodus—of an Hebraic—Semitic people, once slaves in Egypt; and of a Joseph-Imhotep in Egypt; and of a Moses; and also, centuries later, of the Hebrew people conquering the land of Canaan, followed by their Kings: Saul, David and Solomon. Thus, there is solid extra-biblical evidence—that a slave people-Israelites, managed, somehow, to really leave from Egypt and settle in Canaan-Palestine. The Bible's Exodus saga is the in-between story of how the slave-people escaped. Is there anything to create disbelief?"

"11. A logic statement: the wreckage strewn along the ridge pathway off the shore of Saudi Arabia, seven miles away, argues that the chariots, horses and men got there by their own volition—boats or sea currents certainly didn't carry them to where they are today. So, how did they get there? The Bible says the charioteers traveled voluntarily along the ridge-path—chasing Israelites—who seemed to be crossing in safety. Is there any other explanation, plausible or even implausible?"

Serah walked to where she had been sitting, took a drink from her coffee cup, then went back to the lectern. She glanced at Professor Barrett—who raised his eyebrows, then nodded.

"Summarizing," Serah said, "even though the ridge pathway is thousands of feet above the bottom of the Gulf, it is still hundreds of feet below sea level—today. If we assume the Israelites—or whoever was the Egyptian quarry—were never there, then there would be no inducement for the Egyptian charioteers to travel so many miles along the ridge path, away from Egyptian territory. Or, if we assume that 3500 years ago, the water level of the Gulf was much lower, or the ridge path higher, so it was at or even above sea level, then there is no explanation for the coral-covered chariot wreckage? The bible says 'walls of water were held back by an East wind—which then collapsed, drowning the Egyptian charioteers'—but that requires belief in a 'miracle' having occurred—the water being held back for the Israelites, but then collapsing to drown the Egyptians! Other than an initial ridge-path at sea-level enabling the Israelites to escape, then an Earthquake shaking down the ridge-path level so as to drown the Egyptians, is there any other explanation—a fortuitous or non-miraculous, rational one?"

Serah looked around. Several shook their heads in the negative. "In conclusion, a religious believer could argue that the ridge pathway was a topographical 'prop'—set up earlier, perhaps at the beginning of our world—precisely for this event, to demonstrate the omniscience and omnipotence of the world's

Creator. A counter-argument—by a skeptic or non-believer—would be that, while improbable, it was just fortuitous happenstance, that the quarry, let's say the Hebrews, fleeing from the Egyptian chariot army, were just lucky or knowledgeable enough to come upon this ridge path—and somehow the sea level was lower then so the ridge-path was above sea level, then an Earthquake occurred, shaking down the ridge-path to drown the Egyptians, or the East wind was very, very focused, concentrating only on the narrow strip of water above the ridge-path—for the Israelites to escape."

Serah, drew a breath, then, as if in final summary. "So those are the facts. Is there any other spot on Earth that comes even close to matching such a 'land-sea-prop' set-up—completely improbable—but this is the main point, completely essential for the biblical scenario to play out? It's something for us—as 21st century realists—to scratch our heads over."

One by one, the entire group, including the professor, stood up and applauded. Serah, self-conscious, said, "I need something stronger than coffee."

As everyone was preparing to leave, Professor Barrett asked Lawrence to continue with the same subject. "Serah, did a great job on an interesting aspect of what our 21st century data suggests, however, I'd like to nail down artifacts from museums and archaeological sites—validating plagues and mass graves—to see if Science does confirm the Bible."

IVb
Circa 2000 AD, Study Group: Exodus: Undersea Ridge: Encrusted Chariot Wheels: Bones, Men and Horses

Professor Barrett began the session, "At our last meeting, Serah put the issue succinctly, and into the proper context—the remarkable evidence that has been found—much only in the past two decades—about Israelites crossing the Red Sea and the drowning of an Egyptian Chariot army—highlighting the extremely unusual topographical 'set-up' with logic, asking whether such abnormalities can be an indicator of something more than mere happenstance. To refresh our memories of Serah's points: 1) the gigantic size of Nuweiba Beach—the run-off from an average-size, now-dry river bed which meanders between rugged hills; and 2) the ridge pathway—as both the means of their escape and the destruction of the pursuing chariot army. Such a large flat area as Nuweiba Beach would be absolutely essential for a multitude of desperate people to organize themselves and avoid panic—after being strung out for so many, many miles along the twisting, narrow wadi, absolutely vulnerable to attack—and to escape a fast military force of horse-drawn chariots pursuing them. Serah's question—unanswerable dispositively, is a challenging one—is not the improbability of the topographic items—especially their close proximity to each other—extremely persuasive that they appear to be a 'prop set-up'? And—if so, why so? An answer—perhaps arranged by a Creator at the beginnings of Earth itself—for the precise purpose of the Exodus event? Of course, it is unprovable either way, but it seems a valid and interesting 'hypothetical'—calling for personal religious belief and judgment. Such unusual topography—fitting so perfectly with the highly unusual events told in the Bible. It is a fascinating concept!"

Lawrence jumped in, "I've dug up some details that can help flesh out what we know about the area. As had Serah, he took out some notes in power-point format:

• "The inclination of the ridge pathway—it descends from Nuweiba Beach at a 20:1 slope, while the ascent to Saudi Arabia is 14:1, both are manageable slopes for a desperate people on foot."

• "The distance of about seven or eight miles is also compatible with the Bible's time for the Israelites to cross, in a portion of the night, or three to four hours."

• "The diving expedition took place fairly recently, in the spring of 2000; underwater photography was done using both a deep-diving remote-control submersible and individual divers. Also, while Egypt and Saudi Arabia prohibit removal of underwater artifacts, photography is permitted. At least a half-dozen books plus the DVD film show photos of the clumps of chariot wreckage, mostly coral-covered, strewn for miles along the ridge path-way, between Sinai peninsula shore and Saudi Arabia."

• "One artifact is a gilt wheel, providing verification of the Bible's story of the death of Pharaoh in Yam Suf—a four-spoke wooden wheel covered with 'electrum', which is a pale yellow alloy of gold and silver, untouched by coral—which does not adhere to precious metals. The wheel clearly indicates a "royal" charioteer, perhaps Pharaoh. Photography shows it as lying flat; it is circa 1400 BC, which corresponds perfectly to the Exodus period."[256]

• "Also providing a confirming technical point, sensitive underwater metal detectors, were used to verify that the coral-covered wooden wheels had been reinforced with bronze—the Egyptians of the era having developed metallurgical alloying as a process of strengthening their chariot wheels."

• "Of unusual interest was an additional discovery on both the Egyptian and Saudi Arabian shores, described by Dr. Moeller, 'Two identical columns, constructed of the same material and the same size, were found on either side of the Red Sea—Nuweiba Beach, Egypt, and the opposite shore in Saudi Arabia—exactly where the people of Israel are assumed to have crossed.' His explanation, 'King Solomon probably erected them'; he also noted that the Saudi government had recently removed the column on its side and replaced it with an explanatory metal plate." [257]

"Excellent", said the professor, "However—in addition to the implication of the gilt chariot wheel—is there any other extra-biblical evidence regarding biblical references to the death of Pharaoh's firstborn son in the Tenth Plague, and of the drowning of Pharaoh himself with his chariot army. Does anyone know of anything more?"

Ranah cleared her throat, walking to the lectern and projector.

• "Well, there are several historical artifacts which completely support the Bible's stories of both the death of Pharaoh's firstborn son Tutankhamen in the Tenth Plague, and the drowning of Pharaoh. There is a remarkable Amarna letter from the widow of Pharaoh to the King of the Hittites, neighboring people to Egypt at the time, resulting from the death of her Pharaoh husband. The two, together, also resolve a classic historical puzzle, ever since the discovery of the tomb of Boy-King Tut in 1922—why an 18 year old prince is buried in the most lavish of tombs, when the established tradition in Egypt has been that each Pharaoh builds his own tomb during his own lifetime, as a reflection of his life and achievements."

• "The Queen, royal widow of Pharaoh Amenhotep III, writes a most unusual Amarna letter to King Suppiluliumas of the Hittites, 'My husband is dead and I have no son. People say you have many sons. If you send me one of your sons, he will be my husband, [it is] repugnant to me to take one of my servants as husband. Since most ancient times…[has] never happened before. If I had a son should I write to a foreign country…humiliating to me and my country? He, who was my husband is dead and I have no son.'"[206]

• "'Tutankhamen's Tomb,' writes Dr. Moeller in his book, was considered remarkable…no one could understand how a young heir to Egypt's throne…achieved such a magnificent and ornate tomb, a personal death-mask, containing a fabulous display of gold, jewelry, etc.'[197]. Historically, each Pharaoh—especially one with a long reign as ruler of a very wealthy Egypt—built his own tomb while he lived, including what might be needed in his after-life. Yet here—in the largest, most flamboyant and lavish of tombs in all Egyptian history—was buried an eighteen year old prince."

• "Dr. Moeller's book, 'The Exodus Case', provides much solid reference material and advances the most remarkable theory in answer to the question above—that the young Prince Tutankhamen, Pharaoh's first-born son, dies in the Tenth Plague;

then Pharaoh Amenhotep and his chariot army drown in the Red Sea, so his body is lost; therefore the Egyptian court decides to bury Prince Tutankhamen in Pharaoh's available tomb. It all fits." [205]

• "Confirming such a theory is another Egyptian document, 'Young king [is] buried in tomb...originally prepared for Ay.'" [208]

• "Supporting the drowning of the Egyptian charioteers are two statements in the Ipuyer scroll: 'See, he who slept wifeless found a noblewoman...are no more.' This, written as history long afterwards, obviously describes conditions after the loss of the Egyptian army, composed generally of upper-class males: 'See now, the land is deprived of kingship; See, all the ranks, they are not in their place.'"

• "Tel Amarna letters from neighboring cities, dependent for protection on Egypt, ask for troops. 'cities [are] threatened...[we] beg Pharaoh...send troops...but no help comes'. This supports Pharaoh and his army having been lost in the Red Sea, as Egypt would be 'incapable of sending any troops.'; recovery of demoralized Egypt without an army, would be 'the beginning of the end of the 18th dynasty.'" [203]

• "Josephus, the Roman historian born a Jew, with use of the Temple scrolls, quotes Manetho, Egyptian priest circa 300 BC regarding the 'easy conquest" of mighty Egypt by the Hyksos.' [204] —logical if the Egyptian chariot army had been destroyed."

Professor Barrett selected the next session to be on "After the Red Sea Crossing", the Presenter to be Stewart.

V
Circa 1300 BC, Exodus: Marah; Elim; Rephidim; the Amelekite

After the initial reaction of relief—realizing that the immediate threat to their safety had been magically eliminated, that they were now safe and the Egyptian army destroyed—despite a muted joy for the most part, the Israelites experienced an emotional let-down, a draining of energy.

On the first day, Joshua released his army to be with their families, while Moses, Aaron, Joshua and the tribal leaders gathered together on a hill, apart from the people, to assess and analyze their situation. The assistants to the tribal leaders were busy, seeing to any special problems and needs of the people; the messengers were flitting up and back— the final, desperate climb to safety on the ridge-way path, with Egyptian chariots at their heels—had taken a toll of both the wagons and the elderly. The first two days were therefore spent mostly in rest and recovery. However,

Binami and Lansel, with youthful energy and high spirits, were hand in hand, excitedly exploring this new land they were in. On the second day Eliyah and a tallish, slender, reddish-haired girl from the tribe of Dan, Rachisa, found each other; soon the two young couples became inseparable, laughing, and caring and excitedly planning their futures, as young, suddenly free people, confident in themselves, in Moses, and a new life of opportunity and promise.

For a third day, Moses let the Hebrews rest, remaining near where they had gathered after the ridge-way crossing. Gradually, an apprehension now grew among the Israelites, previously knowing only slavery and the orders of masters— that they were now truly free, on their own, in an unfamiliar, frightening world—and completely dependent on their leader Moses.

Finally, with a proclamation to the people to be brave and trust in the Lord, Moses, with his staff in his hand, began walking east-ward, away from Yam Suf, into the unknown. The Israelites were again arranged by tribal family groups, two families abreast behind Moses, then three, then four, growing to seven or eight families side by side, maintaining that width until the stragglers made up the end. Joshua's army, as a loose, protective band, circled about the entire length of the procession of Hebrews. Binami and Chanay, in their fast chariot, continued to scout ahead and on both sides of the procession of Israelites—which composed essentially, the entirety of all the living Hebrew peoples in the world: old, young and in-between, with their possessions.

On the third day of travel, the water pouches of the Israelites were nearing empty, bringing new complaints of thirst. They then came upon a flat plain called "Marah", where existing wells could be seen, already dug in the ground. However, the water was bitter—and the people cried out to Moses, "Better we should have died in Egypt."

Binami, with Chanay—the first to discover the wells and to taste of the bitter water—then saw Moses take a branch from a tree and throw it into the well—then drink of the water—followed by Aaron, then the tribal leaders. Then the Hebrews took branches of that tree and threw them into all the wells—and then they all began drinking, filling their water pouches and watering their cattle. Binami, who before, had found the well-water to be undrinkably bitter, now found it sweet—he whispered to Lansel and Eliyah and Rachisa, "Moses has wrought another miracle."

After the Israelites had all slaked their thirst and stored all the water they could in pouches, Moses led the way onward. They then reached an oasis in the desert called Elim, a place of twelve wells and seventy palm trees, where they encamped. But the people then complained again, crying out to Moses for bread and meat, "Better we should have died in Egypt than to die of hunger here in the wilderness."

It had been six weeks since they had departed Egypt. Binami, having seen how Moses had time and again saved the Hebrew people, felt discouraged, trying in vain for a toning down of the grumbling. Standing with Chanay and Joshua, he saw Moses' face darken with anger at the torrent of complaints—he saw Moses lift up his staff and proclaim to the tribal leaders, "This night they will have plentiful meat, and also bread." Moses then stormed away to be alone.

As dusk fell, there arose the sounds of birds, drowning out all else; they came, completely darkening the sky. In the morning, the ground was covered with quail, in such quantities that every Hebrew gathered as many as was wanted. The ground was also covered with a dew-like substance, which tasted like a wafer of coriander seed and honey. It was "manna" they were told, a bread-like food, and they would be able to collect it every day, the amount gathered would miraculously become exactly enough to feed one Hebrew for one day—and on Friday, enough for two days, so there would be no need to gather manna on the Sabbath. Manna would become the bread-like mainstay of the Hebrew people for the entire duration of their wanderings in the desert and wilderness.

Adjusting to the dryness of the desert, Binami and his friends had adapted to the constant need for water, rationing their supplies; however for the large multitude of Israelites, especially the young, the elderly and those ill, soon could be heard again the cries unto Moses for water. They had come to a place called Rephidim, near Mount Horeb, the highest mountain in the area, which loomed in the background. On a hill before them was a tall boulder, its top as high as a bowman could wing an arrow—it was bare, not a bush or tree grew upon it—it was solid stone.

Binami, with Joshua, Chanay and a select handful of Joshua's warriors, stood guard around Moses as the outcries of the people increased. Binami then saw Moses' face darken with rage and heard him say to Aaron, "The Lord has told me to but speak to the rock to get water, but these people—" Then Moses' voice became a roar, so the Hebrews below could hear, "Ye Israelites are a rebellious people." With that, Moses lifted his staff and struck the huge boulder. Binami could see Aaron gasp in shock, *making a gesture as if to withhold Moses's arm. But Moses struck the boulder again.*

There was an ear-splitting "cra-ak" as of the shattering of something gigantic—and suddenly the single rock was split—becoming two shafts. Between them was now a space, the width of a man's shoulders, smooth and constant for the complete height of the shafts. Then, at the bottom, from the center of the split, came the sound of gushing— and water began spouting from the rock—a constant flow, widening to a stream as it cascaded down the hill to the wildly joyous Israelites below. Moses stalked off to be alone, Aaron trailing him, followed by Joshua and his soldiers at a respectful distance.

Using both hands to cup his fill—the water tasting cool and sweet—Binami later filled his pouch and sought out his friends, to tell them of this latest Moses miracle.

His people now sated with meat and slaked of thirst, Moses led the Israelites onward. Although there had been numerous skirmishes between Joshua's army in their defense of straggling Hebrews against Amelekite raider bands, there had not been a clash of major forces or a pitched battle. Now, however, Joshua's scouts told Moses that directly confronting the Israelites, blocking their continued progress, was a formidable Amelekite army.

A large plain was nearby, with a central rocky promontory to which Moses led Joshua, most of his army following—only a small contingent had been assigned to remain with the Hebrew people in a nearby field. "There", cried Moses, pointing to the promontory, "will I be tomorrow, my arms uplifted to heaven, to pray for your success. Defeat these murderers of our weak and helpless."

At dawn, the next day, came the attack. Alongside Moses on the promontory were Joshua and Chur, husband to Moses' sister, Miriam. Joshua's army encircled the promontory, several circles deep of soldiers; Binami and Eliyah were side by side in the outer ring. That outer circle then positioned their shields, edge to edge, in a solid ring of defensive protection, holding spears in their right hands.

With a blast of a ram's horn and shouts of defiance, the large army of Amelekites descended upon the Hebrews, encircling Joshua's forces.

Joshua, as military commander, had taken advantage of the combat training given Binami by the Pharaoh's guards, schooling in spear, sword and shield—but refining and expanding the practice to suit the needs of an army primarily concerned with protecting a traveling civilian population. Now, however, they were arranged in a solid defensive ring of shields, spears at the ready, surrounding and protecting Moses, Joshua and Chur on the promontory.

The Amelekites attacked self-assuredly, throwing their spears and hacking away at the ring of shields—the Hebrews mostly parrying the thrusts. However, due to over-confidence, when a neck or chest or arm or shoulder was exposed, a quick thrust often drew blood, some-times the wound being mortal. The Amelekites over-aggressiveness was providing openings—the Hebrews, careful, defensive, waited for an opportunity to strike. Fallen soldiers and blood soon covered the ground, two Amelekite for each Hebrew.

As time passed, the arms of the warriors grew weary, their weapons heavy—now three, then four Amelekites fell for each Hebrew. But then, the arms of Moses began drooping.

With a prolonged blast from a ram's horn, the Amelekites charged anew, concentrating on the weakest section of the

Hebrew circle—Moses arms were sagging—the Hebrew protective circle gave way—then broke apart, the circle of shields had yielded—it was now mostly individual combat, one or two Hebrews against three to four Amelekites.

Binami and Eliyah had developed and practiced an approach to open combat that had been very effective when confronting a group of Amelekites on an open field—back to back, so they were invulnerable to attack from the rear—Binami with shield and sword, Eliyah with shield and spear. When an adversary facing Binami seemed susceptible to a spear thrust, he called out to Eliyah, and as one, they pivoted a half-turn to the right—Eliyah, poised for the spear-thrust-target; then, when Eliyah would call out, together, they pivoted a half-turn to the left—and a sword-slash-target would be open for Binami from a drooping shield or sword-arm. The vulnerability of a neck slash was almost always mortal, the blood-flow unstoppable; a spear piercing under a raised arm, between the ribs, could find the heart. Binami and Eliyah had slipped into their back-to-back routine, Eliyah with spear, Binami now taking up his sword. A deadly team, they moved as one, the slightest opening of an adversary, and he soon lay bleeding on the ground.

On the promontory, Joshua and Chur now placed a stone under Moses to give him support, then each raised and propped up an arm of Moses—and a surge of renewed energy and vigor and confidence spread through the Hebrew army—parrying then slashing —parrying, parrying, then thrusting.

Steadily Binami and Eliyah moved through the Amelekites, leaving behind a trail of crumpled bodies. Joshua, catching sight of their progress, called out their names above the clamor and the shrieks and moans—

encouraging them to seek out the King of the Amelekites. "To the right", called out Joshua. Binami sneaked a look, seeing the King on his chariot, surrounded by his elite guard. With a grunt to Eliyah, the two wheeled as one, leaving their adversaries and moved toward the King. Two of his guards, both a head taller than the Hebrews, were engaged; Binami suddenly dropped and swung his sword below the Amelekite shield, slashing the leg of his foe. The man screamed in pain and crumpled. His comrade, distracted, dropped his shield and Eliyah instantly thrust his spear into his chest. As he now cried out and fell, the Amelekite King, only two spear lengths away and seeing his two giant guards vanquished so quickly, suddenly whipped his horse and chariot and sped away from his guards— leaving the battle-field. A wild cheer broke out from scores of Hebrew throats. First some, then mauy of the Amelekites threw down their weapons, some huddling together, cowering and lifting their arms in surrender. Many also ran off the field of battle. The Hebrews for the most part, let then go. The ground was bloody with the sIain and wounded. The remnants of Joshua's army gathered around Moses, Joshua and Chur on the promontory—jubilant that the day-long battle was finally over—and that they had won.

Tired, bruised and sore, both Binami and Eliyah quickly found Lansel and Rachisa, who couldn't stop kissing them, in their happiness at seeing them alive and whole. Each had suffered only a few shallow cuts, which the girls happily treated with olive oil,

Finally, the sun set on a memorable day.

V

Circa 2000 AD, Study Group: Exodus; Alkaline Wells, Oasis, Rephidim, the Amelekite

Following the verification of the biblical narrative given by the Egyptian historical records, the group's fascination with the undersea artifacts of chariot wheels, had not waned despite the passing of the month.

"I just can't get over it," said Serah, "wreckage of chariots from the 18th Dynasty—3500 years ago—and found so recently—just a decade ago." She paused, then added. "And the world doesn't seem to take any notice." She shook her head.

Avi, said, "That's the way it is with modern America—this stuff isn't exciting—not like rap concerts or pop records or political correctness or celebrity stars."

Lawrence, joined in, "What I found interesting was that the half-dozen books I've seen, all seem to have many of the same chariot wheel photos. Isn't there some sort of copyright protection that prohibits authors from using someone else's work?" He looked around the group.

Serah explained, "Copyright law is very solid, but there's an exemption called 'Fair Use'". She went on, clearly familiar with the subject, "While the fundamental premise of the law of copyright is to protect intellectual property against infringement—meaning the owner has exclusive rights to protected work—the Copyright Act of 1976 also established exceptions to those rights—the most significant being 'fair use'. Section 107 of the Copyright Act limits exclusive rights of copyright owners for purposes such as criticism, teaching, scholarship research and general pursuits of social value—all derived from the constitutional objective of promoting progress in science and useful arts. Even photographs can be used sometimes, although, in this instance, permission may have been obtained from the major exploratory expedition, which used robot submersibles as well as divers—and photos of these pieces of wreckage are now well-known and exposed."

"What's so remarkable," said Ranah, "is that these many different pieces of wreckage are found strewn along that ridge today, in year 2010—just think what must have been swept over the sides by storms during these thousands of years—lost in mile-deep water!"

"Or buried in the undersea silt." added Lawrence.

"Did everyone note the statements in several of the books, that there are no other similar clumps of coral-covered chariot wheels anywhere" asked Dana, "even in the same Gulf of Aqaba?"

"I've got a question," said Ranah. "The Bible says that the number of Jews who came to Egypt with Joseph and his father Jacob, was sixty-six. Then, 430 years later, the Bible says there were six hundred thousand men, so maybe a total of a million and a half to two million Jews at the Exodus. Is that a reasonable growth or is it biblical exaggeration?"

"Well" said Bethe, the mathematician of the group, "There is biblical comment that the Hebrew word for 'thousands' could also mean 'clan', thus significantly reducing the number. However, even if it is in the million to two million range, it's not unfeasible—if one assumes an agrarian society built about family, probably marriages occur during the middle to late teens, and an average generational time-period would be perhaps twenty-five years or so, thus totaling seventeen generations. It works out at an average replacement number of about 2-to-1 or about 4 children per couple—not unfeasible. So you can have over a million and a half."

"Yeah," said Avi. "The size of the Hebrew people, down through the ages, is quite a commentary on humanity's intolerance of Jews—3500 years ago, when the world's population was tiny, there were a million-and-a-half Hebrews; then at the time of Rome, fifteen hundred years later, it's eight million; then two thousand years later, in 1939—after pogrom after pogrom in Europe, it not-quite doubles to fifteen million; but then six years later, in 1945, after the Holocaust murders of six million—and by the most culturally-sophisticated countries: Germany, France, European countries—it's down to nine million. Today, over six decades later, it's again only about fourteen or fifteen million!"

The silence among the group was drawn out and painful, a few sighed.

Finally Lanit asked, "How solid is the number of eight million Jews at the time of the Romans, where does it come from?"

Rick answered, "The noted historian, Paul Johnson, in his book, "A History of the Jews".

Professor Barrett changed the subject, speaking somberly. "OK, let's stick to the sequences of the Exodus story—what has been or can be affirmed by science or expeditions and what cannot. So, after the crossing of Yam Suf and the destruction of the Egyptian chariot army, the Israelites come to a place of bitter water, Marah."

"That seems to be verified," said Lanit, "There are many photos of a field with alkaline dry wells in Saudi Arabia, near the crossing site. Anyone know enough about chemistry—is there a tree which chemically offsets alkalinity and can make the water sweet?" Everyone shrugged.

"Well, that's something we'll have to look into." said the professor.

"Next on the way is the oasis of Elim, with many water wells and palm trees," continued Lanit, "Now that seems pretty well established—apparently it's now a thriving Arabian town called Al Bad.[244] And a large plain is nearby, with a rocky hill in the center—matching the biblical account in location, size, and a central promontory where the biblical battle with the Amalekites took place—Moses with uplifted arms, being supported, for the Jewish victory to be achieved." [245]

"How about that giant rock that was split at Rephidim?" asked Rick. "On the Internet I saw some adventurers posing in the gap—and that split rock is almost enough to make a believer of anyone. That six story double-shaft boulder, with a constant gap the entire height, looks exactly like what the Bible says happened—or it was made by the Disney Studios in Hollywood. I plan a trip to the Mid-East soon and, along with the chariot wheels, my primary motivation is to see that split boulder."

"When you do," said Avi, "Don't forget to look for water erosion in the base—many writers have commented on it."

The professor cleared his throat, "Also, there's 'manna' called out in the Bible, surely a miraculous item of bread-like food. Does anyone have anything in today's science and knowledge to throw light on it?" He looked around the room. Everyone shook heads in the negative.

"Well," said Avi, "I read somewhere that the hardened sap of the tamarisk tree, a common tree there, tastes like bread."

Ranah spoke up, "OK, these are some things on which we haven't a clue—on those we either reject the Bible's take on it or we don't."

"Yes," said the professor, "manna and a tree that can neutralize alkali—let's see if anything can be dug up on those items. But even if we find nothing, our batting average for verification of the Bible as history—and for many extreme items, seems to be pretty high." Many nodded.

"How about the battle with the Amelekite?" asked Serah.

Lanit started the discussion, "Well, as I said, there is a likely candidate field in that locale, a flat and open meadow with a promontory on it, which matches the biblical account. Also, the Bible tells of the Israelites building an altar to sacrifice to God after their victory—and there are two altars in the vicinity of Mount Jabal Al Lawz—seemingly Mount Sinai." She added, "And those altars are really something—decorated with drawings of Egyptian bulls with their unusual horns—and in Saudi Arabia, hundreds of miles from Egypt. I would say, that's pretty good validation of the biblical account. The business of the Hebrews winning or losing being dependent on Moses uplifted arms being supported, seems to be just normal cheer-leading psychology."

"But about the Amelekite," said Avi, going back to Serah's question, "well, per the Bible, their origin is with the first patriarch, Abraham—when Sarah couldn't conceive, she gave him her maid-servant Hagar as a concubine, which seems to have been the custom then—and Ishmael was born."

"Great custom," said Stewart.

Avi ignored the comment, "—later Sarah had Isaac—so Ishmael was the original Arab, his descendants were the Amelekites of the Exodus, as well as the Arabs of today, now followers of the Muslim religion."

Lanit added, "Extremely interesting is the instruction from God in the Bible—that the Amelekites are to be killed, every one, because of their murdering the helpless and innocent—to 'utterly blot out the Amelekite from under the heavens'". She added, "and in today's world, it is their descendants, Muslim suicide bombers, the Jihadists, who are the extremist killers, not only of the 'Infidels' that they target in the world at large, but even their own fellow co-religionists, everywhere. The Bible's words are, 'War with Amelekite—from generation to generation'."

There was a long silence.

As they began to leave, Professor Barrett, established the next session to cover Mount Sinai and the Golden Calf, Bethe to be Presenter.

VI
Circa 1300 BC, Mount Sinai; The Golden Calf

Binami, Lansel, Eliyah and Rachisa were feeling restless. It was the second day after the battle with the Amelekites, and having fully recovered, they were now anxious to see this 'Mountain of God' that everyone talked about. It was told that Moses' father-in-law, High Priest of Midian, a distinguished-looking man of many years, had arrived in their camp bringing his daughter, Moses' wife and their children to join Moses; and that he had advised Moses about setting up a system of lower and higher court judges, to rule on various level issues, those which did not warrant Moses as arbiter.

Checking with Joshua and that they had free time, the four decided to scout out the area leading to the mountain, looming in the distance. Rumbles of thunder were frequently heard, and lightning played at the mountaintop, streaking through the clouds. Both girls were frightened at the noise and display, so they all decided to remain on the flatland. They came upon a large, well-watered meadow in a valley surrounded by rolling hills, which, all agreed, would be ideal for the Israelites with their cattle. At the end of the day, the men reported their finding to Joshua, then returned to their families.

It was now in the third month after they had left Egypt. After the departure of his father-in-law, Moses began the march to the valley that Binami and his friends had found; there the people settled. At the center of the camp, a large tent was erected for meetings, then the tents of Moses and Aaron; surrounding them, the tents of the tribal leaders, positioned in the birth order of the original brothers; the tribes were then settled behind each leader.

Frequently thunder and lightning could be heard and seen at the mountain top, keeping the people in a constant state of foreboding and fear.

Full of youthful energy, Binami and Lansel walked early each morning, enjoying the air's freshness and their togetherness, planning their future—one morning they spied Moses walking up the mountain, alone, staff in hand; as he climbed, it seemed that a part of the cloud came down from the top of the mountain to meet and engulf him. As the young couple watched Moses disappear, Binami felt Lansel's shoulders quiver as if with cold—he put his arm around her and she buried her face in his shoulder.

Binami was on patrol with Chanay at the foot of the mountain when they saw Moses finally come down. Aaron and the leaders bowed their heads as they greeted him— then Moses took Aaron into the large meeting tent. Shortly thereafter, Aaron came outside and brought in the tribal leaders. After a long while, they all departed, then criers were sent to all the people: Moses had met with the Lord; in three days time, the Israelites would be told of the Lord's Commandments. But now, they were cautioned—no-one was to go beyond the foothills, upon the mountain for fear of death; it was holy ground and the Israelites were to surround it with mound-piles of rocks, all around the mountain as warning markers. Immediately, Joshua called for Chanay and his chariot, and his soldiers began collecting rocks to build the piles—as high as a man—placed at an arrows-flight distances apart—circling the entire Mountain of God.

The people were also told that they must purify and sanctify themselves, to wash their clothing, and to abstain from personal physical relations between man and wife for three days.

At the end of the three days, Moses led the people to the foot of the mountain, to the border-line of rock piles. Suddenly, from the mountain-top, thunder rumbled and lightning crackled, causing all, even stalwart men, to tremble. The mountain-top then became ablaze with fire and smoke, and a voice of thunder shook the mountain; it reverberated to quake the ground, everyone falling to their knees, some prostrating themselves, "I am the Lord, your God, Ye shall have no other Gods before me." The Israelites covered their ears in fear.

Then, again Moses climbed the mountain, this time with Aaron, Joshua and seventy elders, those comprising the Sanhedrin, or Judicial Council that Moses had established. Binami and Eliyah were with Chanay at the foot of the mountain; they watched all but Moses stop halfway up, only Moses continuing until the clouds again descended to engulf him.

As night fell and Moses had not reappeared, Aaron, Joshua and the tribal leaders came down, then joined their families as the people dissembled back to their tents. Everyone spoke in hushed tones that Moses was meeting with God. Only Chanay, Binami and Eliyah kept a vigil at the foot of the mountain, taking turns for the night watch.

The next morning Moses came down from the clouds, Binami and the others trailing him to the camp. Aaron and the leaders came up to him—Binami and the soldiers, a respectful distance behind, watching as they conversed. Soon they disbursed —to gather the people and lead them to the foothills of the mountain,

An overwhelming blast as of a gigantic ram's horn shook the mountain, and all the Hebrews covered their ears and fell on their knees, Then a voice of thunder intoned nine additional Commandments: "Honor the Sabbath to keep it holy; Honor thy father and mother; Thou shalt not kill; Thou shalt not commit adultery; Thou shalt not steal; etc."

Binami and Eliyah, now together with their girls, listened in awe and wonderment, the rules were simple and sensible, a reasonable basis on which to live a good life—Ten Commandments that they must uphold: how they must comport themselves with their families, with each other and even how to treat strangers in their midst—but primarily that they must worship no other Gods, nor make false idols. They were to build an altar of natural stone and sacrifice upon it to the God of Moses.

Binami watched in awe: Moses commanded the people to do so, and they built a stone altar; he took Aaron and the tribal leaders and they built twelve pillars, one for each tribe. The next morning, Moses sacrificed a bullock on the altar, sprinkling its blood upon the leaders, the elders, and the nearby people. Moses, with help from Aaron and Joshua, then climbed a rock and looked down upon the Hebrew *people, massed before him. He pointed to the sprinkled blood, his voice thundering, "This is the blood of your Covenant with God. Do you accept this covenant?" He said it three times. "Do you accept this covenant? Do you accept this covenant with God?"*

Binami and Eliyah stood, shoulder to shoulder, their free arms about the waists of Lansel snd Rachisa—all standing as tall as possible: with one voice, along with the cries of the entire Hebrew multitude, they shouted, "We do accept! We do accept! We do accept!"

The next morning, Moses went up to the Mountain of God—and was not seen again for forty days and nights. When he finally came down, his face was radiant, glowing, his beard and hair pure-white. He was carrying two stone tablets, chiseled with words,

But the Israelites had not waited patiently for their leader to return. As day after day had passed into weeks, some had grown fearful that Moses would not come back—they cried out to Aaron, "We know not what has befallen Moses—we must pray for him—make for us gods to which we can pray!"

The voices of doubt and fear grew among the Hebrews— day by day —from a few to many —until it worried Binami that so many of the Hebrews were demanding idols to pray to and worship.

The two girls nervously whispered their fears to Binami and Eliyah, that perhaps this fierce God on the mountain, had, in anger, killed Moses. "No, no, no." said Binami, "I have seen the great miracles that Moses has performed through the God of the Mountain—God would not harm Moses." But despite the confidence in his voice, Binami did have doubts, which grew as the weeks became a month and more, with no sight of Moses.

Binami also saw the doubts growing in Joshua, and that even Aaron was becoming disheartened. Finally, he heard Aaron yield to the growing clamor of the multitude, now pleading daily for new gods to ease their fears. "Give me your golden jewelry," he finally said, "and I will make for you a golden idol to worship."

Binami watched in apprehension as the Israelites heaped their jewelry at the feet of Aaron: wrist bracelets and finger rings and ear-rings, many of the golden baubles that the Egyptians had given them to hasten their departure from Egypt. Sadly, Binami and Chanay and Joshua saw Aaron assemble the most skilled workmen among the Hebrews, watched as they melted the gold and began crafting—a golden calf.

Joshua, almost broken in spirit, gathered his faithful soldiers and left the encampment, remaining at the foot of the mountain to await Moses' return.

Finally, after forty days and nights, Moses reappeared from the clouds.

As Moses came closer, Binami could see he was carrying two tablets of stone, one in each hand, on them carvings, marking out words. But, as Moses descended, strange sounds could be heard coming from the camp below— people singing and rejoicing. Moses abruptly slowed his pace and stopped, waiting for Joshua and his honor guard to draw near.

As Joshua spoke quietly to him, Moses' face darkened in anger. Swiftly now, Moses descended and stormed into the camp—everyone in his path, even Aaron, slinking away.

Then Moses saw the golden calf, a half-dozen Hebrews, male and female, kneeling before it. With a shout of hurt and anger, Moses flung the two stone tablets to the ground— shattering them. Then Moses, in anguish, crumpled to his knees, his shoulders shaking with sobs that everyone could hear. The revelers before the golden calf swiftly quieted, then slunk away. Aaron and some elders, first knelt, then prostrated themselves before the collapsed figure of Moses. Binami watched the tragedy unfold, hardly daring to breathe.

After a time, Moses lifted his head, sighed deeply, looked around and signaled Joshua to help him up, Chanay, Binami and the others respectfully staying behind Joshua. Moses, ignoring Aaron who was now pleading for his brother to look at him, pointed to the golden calf and, in a hoarse voice, ordered Joshua and his men to smash it to pieces. Binami, Joshua and the others jumped to do so; Moses then ordered them to grind the pieces into dust, and they did so; Moses then ordered them to mix the dust with water from a nearby stream, and they did so; Moses then ordered them to force the idolators to drink the mixture, and—with swords in hand—Joshua's men then forced the Hebrews who had worshipped the calf to drink.

Moses, then ordered the tribe of Levi, which had remained aloof from the golden calf, plus Joshua's army, to stand behind him. He then called out to the multitude, "Those who are on the side of the Lord. come to me."

Aaron, the tribal leaders and almost all of the populace swiftly moved behind Moses. Moses then—in a quiet but firm voice—ordered the tribe of Levi and Joshua's loyal soldiers to take up swords and to slay the Hebrews who had violated the First Commandment. As they drew their swords, Moses exhorted them, "You are not to have pity for these idolators—your swords are the instruments of our Lord God, who is fierce with anger at this apostasy—what they have done. You are meting out justice against the enemies of God."

Binami and Eliyah were numb, weary in spirit and body—after their participation in the killings of hundreds of fellow Israelites—those of insufficient faith. As Binami held a weeping Lansel in his arms that night, words seemed inadequate—he could only whisper words of comfort, "This shall pass."

VI

Circa 2000 AD, Mount Sinai; Mounds of Stone; Altars with Egyptian Aphis Bull Paintings

Professor Barrett opened the next session, "OK, so now Moses has led the Israelites to Mount Sinai. Bethe, ready to go on?"

Bethe nodded and went to the lectern, holding a sheaf of papers: "It seems that Mount Jabal Al Lawz or Lodz, in Saudi Arabia, is the 'real McCoy'—all those cited books and the Internet are full of photos that seem to satisfy the descriptions in the bible for Mount Sinai. I've got them listed:

• "There is a scorched, darkly discolored top in all the photos, yet it is a granite mountain with nothing combustible, not even trees. Climbers say the granite at the top seems to have been molten—which agrees with the Bible's statement of fire and flame at the top. [253]

• "There's a cave, as where Moses and Elijah hid their faces to avoid looking at God—local Bedouins call it 'Elijah's cave'"[249];

• "The Bedouin name for the mountain is Jabal Musa, "Mountain of Moses".[254]

- "Sketches and photos by visitors show broken sections of round stone pillars at the base—which tie in with the twelve pillars that the Bible says Moses erected for the twelve tribes." [251]
- "There's a line of stone mounds running around the mountain. They are described as eight to ten feet in diameter and spaced about a third or fourth of a mile apart, curving about both sides of the mountain and separating it from the flat plain. Of course, surrounding the whole area today, is a fourteen foot barbed wire fence, with Arabic signs calling it an Archaeological Site." [252]
- "There are also two very large stone altars decorated with petroglyph drawings depicting the uniquely-horned Egyptian Aphis bulls;" [250]
- "One book describes gold dust being found in the soil near a brook—the author claiming it as proof of the biblical story of the Golden Calf, which Moses broke up and had ground into dust which was cast into the brook—then forcing the idolaters to drink of it." [248]

Dana interrupted, "You know, using 21st century facts and logic, these things are really there, so there's a question—who would have built them in Saudi Arabia, and when, and why: the piles of rocks around the mountain; those altars; and those twelve pillars? Other than as told in the Exodus story of the Bible, can anyone come up with a reasonable, non-biblical, explanation?"

Bethe wasn't done with her listing, "Wait, there's something else about the topography—the question of how the large number of Hebrews survived for perhaps a year. Well," she said, "there is a large flat, well-watered valley just off the base of Mount Jabal Al Laws, which is perfectly suitable for a long encampment for hundreds of thousands of people, even with herds. The valley is 25 miles long and one-and-a-half miles wide,[246] and is even contiguous to a vaster plain, fifteen by seven miles. There is abundant water and vegetation for a multitude, even for a long encampment—and as also for what would be required for Jethro's herds, tended forty years earlier by the young Moses." [247]

"Well," summarized the professor. "It appears that there is topographical consistency with the biblical description of Mount Sinai.

Avi cleared his throat, "As a commentary upon the pervasive power of media propaganda, and the conventional wisdom of what the world believes—rather than truth and fact—are these well-advertised tours of Mount Sinai, taking pilgrims or adventurers to lower Sinai Peninsula, although completely devoid of any topographical attributes of the biblical Mount Sinai. Meanwhile, here is Jabal Al Lawz in Saudi Arabia—with everything the Bible talks about—described in a dozen books and easily seen on the Internet. What a sad reality!" He shook his head, others doing the same.

Serah laughed. "Well, that puts us in a unique category—more knowledgeable than almost all of the leaders of society—our brain-washed elite—whose erroneous conventional wisdom is that the Bible is essentially only myth! Hah!"

The professor said, "OK, we're about done with Exodus. I'll do the wrap-up for the next session."

VII
Circa 1300 BC, Scouts; Rebellion; 40 Years Wandering; Deaths of Aaron and Moses

The atmosphere about the camp was full of gloom for many weeks after the Golden Calf episode and the killings of the idolaters—many of the Israelites had known some of those slain; the families who had lost members felt shamed, and moved to isolate themselves at the outskirts of the camp.

Binami had watched Moses go up to the mountain-top again, but now, everyone knew he would return, the general feeling being that he would be away for another lengthy period. Binami noted Aaron's attitude of withdrawal, essentially removing himself as second to Moses— spending much time in prayer, meeting only with his Levites. This benefited Binami—Joshua had assumed responsibility with Aaron's withdrawal and Moses' absence, and now devoted himself exclusively to tribal leader problems—Chanay had become the operating military commander; in turn, promoting Binami as his lieutenant.

Meanwhile, Binami and Lansel, and Eliyah and Rachisa, had begun planning their marriages—lifting their spirits along with all who knew them—with joy and the excitement of their optimism about their futures.

After the mourning period had passed for those Hebrews who had been killed, Binami could feel an increasing confidence in the spirits of the people. Many able-bodied men had joined the Hebrew armed forces, and the days were busy with patrols and constant military exercises. It became clear to Binami that Joshua was preparing for what lay ahead, anticipating many hostile peoples to be encountered and overcome.

Moses finally returned—after exactly forty days and nights, and carrying two new tablets of stone on which symbols of the Ten Commandments were carved. Binami, part of the welcoming group of Joshua, Chanay and the tribal leaders, saw that his face shone even more than before. Aaron had remained quietly in the background, restricting himself to purely religious matters.

Finally came the day of joy and happiness—the marriages of Binami and Lansel, Eliyah and Rachisa, plus scores of other couples in a combined ceremony. Moses himself and Aaron officiated. There were seven days of celebrating for the entire people of Israel after so many months of fear, uncertainty and struggle. Now the attitude became one of hope and a joyous future.

As the camp settled into a commonplace routine, in addition to the constant military practice, Binami found pleasure in a new activity instituted by Moses —which reminded him of his tutelage under Manthro in Egypt.

Moses began giving detailed lessons from the learning he had received from the Lord: about building a Sanctuary, a Tabernacle and an Ark of the Covenant; about the laws of the Sabbath; of circumcision; of ritual cleanliness; of women's monthly periods of impurity; of death and dead bodies and purification and mourning periods; of religious standards and purity for food, what could be eaten and what not. There were laws about proper respect for parents, requisite behavior with family and associates, even strangers; that during harvest, the corners of fields were to be left for the gleanings of the poor and strangers, also the droppings from fruit trees. These rules of behavior and morality were taught, first to Aaron and the tribal leaders, elders, and military officers including Binami, then in turn, to all the people.

To build the tabernacle, the most expert artisans and skilled workmen among the people were recruited, along with all the materials needed: specially stained wood, precious stones, gold for plating the holy Ark and woven goods for curtains, To carry the holy articles with them wherever the Israelites would travel, designs of rings and staves were included. Gradually, the Tabernacle and the Ark of the Covenant were crafted and assembled, and the place for the Sanctuary was erected —the Levites, under Aaron, taking control of this symbolic prayer site of the Lord God of the Israelites.

With hours spent each day in combat training with the citizen-soldiers, Binami gradually became aware of an attitude of concern growing into fear among the populace, "We hear there are giants in the land that Moses is taking us *to—they will kill us." and "Better we should be slaves in Egypt!" Binami passed on the information to Chanay, from him to Joshua, then to Moses himself—that the people wanted scouts to be sent, to see what the land and its occupants were like, and to bring back specimens of the fruit and products. In Binami's hearing, Moses exploded, "The Lord has already scouted this land for us—how dare this stubborn people ask this?"*

But as time passed, and the fear and grumblings grew, Moses finally consented to a scouting expedition, one scout from each of the twelve tribes. The leaders of the mission were Joshua and Caleb from the tribes of Ephriam and Judah. The scouts were gone for forty days exploring the land of Canaan, returning with a large cluster of grapes— and with stories of mighty forces against them, of the Canaanites, and Amelikites, and Hittites, and Jebusites, and Emorites—and well-fortified cities —that the Hebrews would not be able to defeat. So reported ten of the scouts to Moses and the elders—that the Israelites could not succeed militarily in conquering Canaan—that they should return to Egypt, even to be slaves again!

Binami's heart sank at hearing such words from the scouts, one after another, ten negative reports. But then came Joshua and Caleb—angry with the ten and their pessimistic reports—instead they roared confidence in themselves and the Lord God to defeat all the peoples of the land. Binami, his heart pounding now, shouted his support of Joshua and Caleb. All eyes were now focused on Moses, whose face was as dark with anger as Binami remembered when Moses had confronted Pharaoh.

Moses stood up, looking at no-one—he closed his eyes, his face growing calm—he became immobile, as if in a trance. *Everyone grew silent, watching. Time passed. Moses stood rock-like.*

Finally Moses opened his eyes—but he looked straight ahead, staring at the horizon. His voice was calm, "This report is evil, showing there is no trust in our Lord God." He paused, "Thus says the Lord—for each day of the forty days, the Hebrew people will wander in the wilderness for one year—until this entire faithless generation is gone—only Caleb and Joshua will live to enter the promised land." Moses then walked away, not looking to the right or left.

A hush was on the multitude. Then Binami saw one of the ten scouts cry out in pain, turn ashen and slump to the ground, then another, and another. Soon all ten were writhing on the ground. In shock, no-one moved to help them. Gradually the ten quieted, lay immobile. Then family members, weeping, took away their dead—for burial outside the camp.

For the mourning period of thirty days, the mood of the Israelites was somber, knowing their destinies, their lifetimes to be wilderness-wandering.

Time passed, and Binami and Lansel had a son whom they named Moses; and Elijah and Rachisa had a daughter they named Daphira. Their happiness in each other and their children made their lives full and rich despite the nagging knowledge of their own futures—feelings of sadness overcome by hope, even confidence, in the futures of their children.

In the first month of the second year of the Exodus from Egypt, the tabernacle was set up—immediately the pillar of cloud of the Lord rose above it—becoming a pillar of fire by night. Binami experienced a flush of exultation. He felt inspired by the thought that the Hebrew people were now ready to be led again by the columns of fire and cloud, the beacons of God, leading them onwards—even for forty years through the desert and wilderness.

Binami, closer to the people through the citizen-warrior training exercises, was the first to become aware of resentment festering among some Hebrews—instigated by jealousy of Aaron and Moses. He reported his observations to Chanay, who passed them on to Joshua and finally to Aaron and Moses—the feelings of the people gradually rising to expressed challenges and open rebellion. Two of the tribe of Reuben, Dathan and Abiram, whose tents were located in the south of the camp, were openly accusing Moses of having appointed himself as leader of the Israelites. And there was Korach, even confronting Moses directly, "I am from the stock of first-born Reuben, and so I am entitled to the Chieftainship. Moses, you take too much upon yourself—our entire congregation is holy. The Lord is in the midst of us all. Why do you raise yourself above the assembly?"

With Moses attempting to ignore such challenges, they only worsened. Soon after, Korach and some of the tribe of Levi, also began challenging Aaron's position as High Priest.

Moses had sent to Datham and Abiram to come up to the Meeting Tent to join with the rebellious Levis, but they ignored his request, "Moses, we will not go up."

Binami and his soldiers watched with growing alarm as Korach assembled 250 men who supported him, mostly from the tribe of Reuben, but some also being learned elders of the Sanhedrin. Binami reported it to his superiors—this was now serious, an openly rebellious force against Moses and Aaron,

Moses hearing of this, fell on his face. Joshua, with Chanay and Binami at his side, said to Moses, "Shall we draw our swords against them?"

Moses shook his head, "No. This is a challenge, not to me, but to the Lord."

Moses then went to Korach's assembly and spoke to them: "In the morning, the Lord will make known his choice, who is holy." He then turned to the Levites who were defying Aaron—each should take his censer vessel and coals, to sprinkle them with incense, and thus to ready them for the Lord's fire—if they would be chosen.

Joshua and his army, including Binami and Elijah, formed a guard around Moses and Aaron, closely watching the playing-out of events. Moses, they saw, was in clear distress and had sunk to his knees; he emitted a cry of pain to the Lord, "Accept not their offering. I have not harmed even one of them."

Moses then rose and sent word to Korach, "You and your congregation on the morrow, all will be before the Lord—and the Levites also, each man with his censer plus coals and incense, and Aaron also—to see who will be chosen by God."

At dawn, the next morning, everyone stood ready, each praying to the Lord to be selected. Binami and Joshua's army surrounded Aaron and the rebellious Levites—250 of the tribe of priests with their censers. Korach, Datham and Abiram, all stood, defiant at the entrance of the Tent of Meetings. The Hebrew people all crowded around, watching with bated breath.

Moses then cried out to the congregation, "The Lord says that all of you who are not with Korach, Datham and Abiram are to withdraw from them."

Many drew back in fear—and Korah, Datham and Abiram, with their families, then went to the entrances of their own family tents.

In a strong voice, Moses then said, "By this you shall know that the Lord sent me to do this thing—It was not I who devised it."

The ground began shaking. All fell to the ground. Binami watched in horror as the earth suddenly opened—beneath Korach, Datham and Abiram—instantly swallowed up, along with their families, their tents and all their possessions. And all of Israel who were near, fled so as not to be swallowed up also.

And as Binami still watched—awe-struck—there came a mighty roll of thunder—and fingers of fire streamed down from the heavens—and, in a flash, all the 250 Levites who had challenged Aaron with their censers were consumed. Then, a thin, single streak of forked lightning, with a single clap of thunder, lit the censer of Aaron.

And so, gradually it became accepted that this generation of Hebrews would be forced to wander in the wilderness for forty years—until a new generation of Israelites had matured; all the males would have their foreskins circumcised—the Israelite people would then be led to their promised land.

And forty years passed —the tribes of Israel had become nomads of the desert for all that time. They had contested with the occupants of the lands who would not let them pass through in peace, or who had withheld water and vegetation—protected by the might and skill of Joshua's army, and the people's belief in Moses and their Lord God— and with the columns of cloud and fire above the Ark of the Covenant which led them. Almost the entire Exodus generation had now been buried along the way.

Moses and Aaron were now very old, walking with difficulty. The Israelites had reached Mount Hor, by the boundary of Edom, east of the river Jordan. Binami and Joshua watched as Moses and Aaron climbed the mountain with their staffs, moving slowly. Aaron was wearing the over-garment of his position as High Priest. Aaron's son Eleazar walked behind them. Tiny figures high up in the mountain, they could still be seen by Binami and the Hebrew people: Moses and Aaron turned to face each other, then embraced. Then Moses lifted the over-garment of the office of the High Priest from Aaron's shoulders and placed it over the head and onto the shoulders of Eleazer. Aaron and Eleazer then embraced. A moment later, Aaron and Moses turned and began climbing higher up the mountain.

After a time Moses returned to sight, followed by Eleazer, now wearing the High Priest over-garment—Aaron had worn that symbol of his position for forty years.

It was proclaimed to the elders and tribal leaders, then to the people, that Aaron had been gathered unto his ancestors, at the age of 123 years—and the Israelites mourned for thirty days.

Joshua still enjoyed the strength of middle age, seeming with endless energy. Chanay had been killed in battle a decade ago—Binami was now Joshua's second-in-command. As such he had been told by Joshua that Moses would not enter the promised land of milk and honey, but was going to die on a mountain east of the river Jordan; that it would be he, Joshua, who would complete Moses' Exodus mission and lead the new generation of Israelites into Canaan. Many battles would be needed to conquer the land—no knowing if Binami would survive. Binami, however, had a soldiers's philosophy, and was content to fight to the death for the life he had been given with Lansel, a life of freedom and children, of miracles witnessed, of leaders to be proud of, and of a Lord to be both feared and worshipped.

The Israelites had now reached the land of Moab—there remained only the crossing of the Jordan River to finally enter into the land so long promised. Knowing that Moses would not be permitted to do so, Binami and Joshua watched in sadness as Moses slowly climbed Mount Nebo—from which he could see the entire land—to which he had brought his people, the Israelites, but which he was not permitted to enter.

It was reported to the people that he had led for forty years, that Moses died there in the land of Moab, on Mount Nebo, at the age of 120 years, with no man knowing where he was buried.

Many decades earlier, Binami had made peace with the knowledge that only a few of his generation, possibly not he or Lansel, would see the land promised by Moses' Exodus adventure—because of the scout reports which had falsely described the occupants as mighty and undefeatable. Binami and Lansel were both content. They had had good lives—they could recall the frightening times of their early years, when Bnai Israel were slaves in Egypt. Since their togetherness, they had looked upon life as a shared *adventure, thus the decades had passed swiftly. Filled with contentment, they still loved each other, and their families, and had enjoyed happiness to the fullest. Together with Eliyah and Rachisa, both now gone, they had raised families of four and five respectively, enjoyed the delights of weddings, of births, even of flint-stone circumcisions of their male babies, They had experienced the deep satisfaction in acquiring wisdom from the teachings of Moses as he had laid out the instructions received so long ago on Mount Sinai. They had mourned the passing of their parents, their siblings and friends, all leaving cherished memories. Their lives had been full and good.*

Now they clasped hands and smiled at their youngest gurgling grandchild—held firmly on Binami's knees, as the father, a sharp flint-stone in hand, was preparing for the circumcision—the mother, apprehensive, was looking away, Lansel was holding a clean cloth dipped in wine to the baby's lips—drawing its attention from the momentary pain. Then it was over, the baby concentrating on the taste of the wine—everyone happy with relaxed anxiety.

In pure joy, Binami laughed heartily. Looking at his Lansel, his eyes beheld a white-haired old woman, her face wrinkled from too many years and too much sun, though still comely. But, in his minds eye, who he saw was the slender, frightened girl of forty years before, at their first embrace—she shivering with apprehension as his arms enclosed and comforted her—as they stood together, with fear and uncertainty—at the threshold of their life's adventure with Moses and the Exodus of their people— freed by miracles from slavery in Egypt —for a better life, a life of freedom, in a land of promise.

VIIa
Circa 2000 AD, Exodus Wrap-up;
40 Years Wandering; the Promised Land

"Well," said Professor Barrett, "We've examined the scientific, archaeological evidence of an Hebraic, Semitic people who lived in Egypt, the Goshen area, in ancient times; also that similar people, centuries later, conquered cities in Canaan; and there is much proof that the Hebrew Kings: Saul, David and Solomon did exist—therefore, in between, these Hebrews had to have exited Egypt, somehow and sometime." He paused, "Thus, there seemingly, is solid, corroborative evidence of the beginning and end to the Exodus story. Science and knowledge also, in just the past decade, have uncovered hard, artifact and iconoclastic evidence of Egyptian chariot wreckage in the Gulf of Aqaba; also, we see an amazing cleft stone boulder; and a Mount Sinai — practically every detail validating the Bible story. What is interesting, as possible challenges to theology, is that we haven't found any real conflicts. However, we do not have a clue about the miracle food 'manna' by which the Hebrews were supposedly sustained for forty years roaming the desert and wilderness; nor do we know if alkaline water can really be sweetened by the bark or sap from a tree."

"Before a final wrap-up—" Lawrence was raising his hand, "—I've run into something that tends to lend scientific credibility to the Exodus story in general." He paused, "In his book, 'The Mountain of Moses', Larry Williams says he hired a scientific research company to analyze areal photos of the Sinai Peninsula and the Gulf of Aqaba, taken by a French satellite. The procedure was a military development, now employed in archaeological research of Earth surfaces—it discriminates subtle differences in heat patterns using special filters on photographic negatives. The analysis reported a clear trail, estimated as being thousands of years old, going to the waters edge, and resuming on the other side of the Gulf of Aqaba. The trail discloses numerous large campsites, continues parallel to the Gulf and then inland to Mt. Jabal Al Laws, with an extremely large campsite nearby. The same analyses for the traditional Mt. Sinai sites in lower Sinai peninsula show much smaller trails, only a few centuries old and with few campsites."

"Just think" said Bethe, "if we could know the life story of a Hebrew who had lived through that Exodus period, sort of like the Amarna letter of Pharaoh's widow or the Ipuwer Papyrus Scroll or the Egyptian chroniclers Manetho and Cheremon—and with our 21st century verification keeping pace. Now, wouldn't that be something?"

"And so," the professor drew a breath, "we've had quite a journey this past, very interesting year, had some fun and learned quite a bit about ancient peoples and Egypt. I wouldn't be surprised if the number of items corroborating the Bible by artifacts and archaeological discoveries that we've found, isn't about a hundred or so—validating a significant percentage of the biblical stories in detail with 21st century reality.

Finally it was time to go. There were a few handshakes and claps on the shoulder by the men, a few, "We must keep in touch" mumblings by women. But the exchanges seemed awkward, too perfunctory and casual, as if something was missing after a shared year-long, intense, intellectual journey.

They left singly, quietly, a few turned after shaking the professor's hand at the doorway—as if to say something—but they only smiled, waved, and were gone.

"It's been great," said a male voice.

VIIb
Circa 2000 AD, Biblical Exodus, 21ˢᵗ Century Verification

The summons from Professor Barrett—for that is what it amounted to—was cursory, emailed the day after their customary third-Thursday sessions:

"Dear Students and Co-Investigators,

Yesterday evening—absent our normal session- was a "bummer" for me—I missed our get-together. Also, I now feel we haven't properly finished off our year-long project, so: next month—third Thursday—7 p.m.—my home—everyone please bring a bottle of champagne—look sharp (I'll be wearing my red bow-tie, short-sleeved shirt, creased pants and moccasins), also be mentally sharp: session subject; "Biblical Exodus, 21ˢᵗ Century Verification," Let's really nail it down. No excuses short of a heart attack. Prof. Barrett"

As Avi would later tell it, on reading the email, Bethe got that "look" on her face, grinned at him and grabbed the phone. The professor wasn't in, so she rapid-fired into the message machine: "Professor, remember my comment at the end of the final session? I'll have a surprise for you. Please have your secretary copy all the power point summaries of our sessions—will pick them up at 3 today."

Professor Barrett, on hearing her message, guffawed out loud, quickly called Bethe's number. Her answering machine responded: "Bethe, I'm guessing what you're up to. Great idea! Looking forward to it. Don't tell others—great surprise for them. Thought you were into arcane mathematics—not fiction. You and Avi have fun. Barrett."

On the Tuesday before the now-final session, Professor Barrett, Bethe and Avi had dinner (at a kosher restaurant) going over their plans. Bethe gave the professor a sheaf of papers which he quickly skimmed, the smile on his face broadening as he read the first paragraph. He clapped the two young people on the shoulders, "Wonderful—I'll read the rest later. This is just fabulous. Congratulations. Now, let's order and eat, then we'll plan the session."

After the meal, as they parted, the professor said, "OK Bethe, you'll start it. Work with my secretary, make seven hand-out copies to distribute to the others, chapter by chapter—no reading ahead for them. After each chapter, I'll take over. I want some real, solid judgment-estimates from all of us as to how much of the biblical narrative we've validated. Great idea and job, this—I'm proud of you two, every one will love it. Come an hour early."

On the evening of the final session, Professor Barrett met all his students at the door, escorting them to the bar where open bottles of champagne were being poured into cocktail glasses. Everyone was neatly but not overly dressed, all eager to learn what was going on. As his grandfather clock toned seven-fifteen, the professor waved them to seats, stepping to the lectern.

"OK, let's begin. Our imaginative Bethe and Avi have done themselves and us all proud. They've written a fictional account of Hebrews living the Exodus experience, the Passover saga—interacting with Moses and Pharaoh—just as told in the Bible." The reactions from everyone were exclamations of pleased laughter. The professor continued, "They'll pass out the first chapter now—then we'll go over the charts of our first sessions, and begin progressively evaluating how much of biblical historicity we've validated by hard 21st century evidence."

Everyone eagerly grabbed the sheets as Avi passed them out—Bethe then began reading aloud: "Chapter 1, Circa 1300 BC, Egypt; the Royal Palace of Pharaoh Dudimose, 36th Ruler, 13th Dynasty". Bethe paused, looking around, and seeing everyone had sheets, she smiled and her voice deepened—as she read the first words of the story, "As Binami, lying flat on the gallery floor, peered down through the open weave of the curtains onto the Throne Room below,—" Bethe stopped, noting everyone was reading by themselves—many chuckling or openly laughing. Bethe slid quietly onto the sofa next to Avi.

As they all finished, putting down their sheets, one by one they lifted their glasses of champagne to Bethe—silent toasts of approval. Looking up from her sheet, Lanit said, "Good writing, I particularly like that touch of implied future romance."

The professor stood up, walked to a large "white-board" and cleared his throat, getting everyone's attention. "OK, now let's get to the business part. Our interest here is not as pious believers—to try to prove whether or not the Bible contains the literal words of a God-Creator, possibly written by humans as inspired writing instruments—but whether or not the biblical tale of the Exodus is historically true. So, while we can enjoy reading Bethe's and Avi's fictional chapters, we now have to review our briefing charts, session by session, point by point—making our individual judgments as to the degree of verification we've unearthed. I've started with a number of questions—as we progress through the chapters, I expect we'll think of many more. We'll accept or reject them by majority vote, including mine. Then we'll all judge each of the questions as to "relative significance" to the overall Passover story, a factor or percentage number, our group average. Then finally, each of us will assign our own individual judgment factor of 'credibility-validation' for each question—using the following four criteria." He wrote them on the white-board;

Credibility-Validation Factor (21st Century Artifacts):

A. Verified beyond reasonable doubt (.9 - 1);
B. Partial verification (.7 - .9);
C. Implied verification (.5 - .7);
D. No verification (0.0).

Laurence raised a hand, "What's that "Relative Significance Factor" you mentioned before?"

The professor answered, "Let's say we can't find anything regarding some biblical passage—for example "manna", supposedly provided miraculously for food every day. So we give it a zero for Credibility-Validation. But, after all, what's the importance of "manna" to the overall Exodus story? There's so much proof that a Semitic people did live as slaves in Egypt for centuries, evidenced by irrefutable archaeological "digs"; then there's the Imhotep-Joseph statue and references to him; then of the Moses story, the high percentages of buried Semitic infants, Pharaoh wanting to kill Moses; etc. And then there are so many Amarna letters of centuries later, verifying that Hebrews lived in Canaan-Israel—thus, there must have actually been an Exodus of Hebrew slaves from Egypt. In addition, the Hebrews would hardly have starved without 'manna', having their cattle for milk and meat; also, there was grain and produce gleaned from the land—their traveling pace during the forty years was relatively slow, the area covered during the four decades not great. So, while there's no proof for "manna", its significance to the overall story should be only a very small per-cent. With the two factors, 'significance' and 'validation', we can rate everything in context—as to both importance to the total Exodus story and also 21st century verification."

As almost all nodded in agreement, the professor handed out a sheet listing his start-up questions.

Questions Seeking Proof:
1. Was Egyptian Imhotep the Joseph of the Bible?
2. Was there a Moses, an Egyptian Prince?
3. Was he a Hebrew, saved from death in infancy?
4. Did a Semitic or Hebrew people live as slaves in Egypt for centuries?
5. Did the plague-miracles occur?
6. Was Prince Tuthanhumen the first child of Pharaoh, killed in the Tenth Plague (Death of the First-born)?
7. Was there an Exodus of the Hebrew people from Egypt?
8. Did Moses lead them?
9. Did they cross Yam Suf (Red Sea)?
10. Did the sea split (perhaps by an East Wind) revealing a traversable under-sea path
11. Did Pharaoh's chariot army drown? Did Pharaoh drown?

12. Are the alkaline wells on the eastern shore of the Gulf of Aqaba the "bitter waters" of the Bible?

13. Is the oasis town Al Bad, the site of "springs and palm trees" of the Bible?

14. Is the story of the Moses splitting a rock for water verified by what can be seen in book photos and on the Internet—a giant cleft rock?

15. Is the story of Mt. Sinai validated as Jabal al Laws in Saudi Arabia?

16. Do the two rock altars verify the biblical account?

17. Do the mounds of stone found surrounding Jabal al Laws verify the biblical account?

18. Do the remnants of twelve stone pillars verify the biblical account?

As the group began looking up from his listing, the professor continued, "We are serious students and pursuers of historical accuracy, so we want to assess the biblical tale—the millions of words that we all have absorbed on this subject this past year—versus what 21st century facts and artifacts have confirmed."

The professor continued, "I've given much thought on how to evaluate our exposure to so many items, from major considerations such as the reality of that undersea path-way and those coral-covered chariot wheels." He looked around. "Any comments by anyone before we proceed?"

Ranah spoke up, "That cleft rock to me, is the most dramatic proof of the general verification of the Bible story, followed by Mount Sinai. A sixty foot-high boulder split with such a constant and parallel gap is just so un-natural, that it truly speaks to abnormal powers involved in this story." There were many grunts of agreement.

Serah coughed, all eyes swinging to her. She spoke quietly but firmly, "As I elaborated in my 'hypothetical', that topography set-up is just overwhelming to me intellectually, so completely essential to the entire Exodus saga—the land-layout first entraps the Hebrews, then it saves them, then it drowns the pursuing Egyptians—and this is all provable by artifacts existing today for any doubting eyes. Even to an atheist and skeptic—which I had always regarded myself as being—it is just extra-ordinary: starting with that undulating dried river wadi between rugged hills—which leads to the mile-sized open beach—thus those pursued by the chariot army were truly 'trapped' just as the Bible phrases it—the only potential for safety was that undersea path-way, built-up by river silt run-off—from a mile-deep sea-floor—to traverse a seven-mile-crossing. Can all that be just shrugged off?" Serah's rising voice emphasized the question—she then continued, "And, there are those coral-covered ancient Egyptian chariot wheels to prove it all—distributed along the under-sea path across seven miles of deep sea! It's just too much to be accepted as 'natural'—yet there it all is—so easily verifiable by doubters."

Everyone was silent, absorbing Serah's words. Then the professor took over in a quiet voice. "There are also considerations such as, 'Did the Nile really turn to blood? Did the staff of Moses really turn into a snake? Did alkaline well-water become sweet? Therefore, let's get started—my secretary, Rosie will join us and help—we're going to dredge up a bushel-full of numbers."

At his words, his secretary emerged from the kitchen area, waving a "hello" to everyone, and going to a small table-chair set up in a corner of the room. On the table was a stack of folders and a computer. She took the top folder and began passing out sheets to each of the group.

"OK," said the professor, "Let's start with the power-point listings of our first session, almost a year ago. Using the list of questions I passed out before, let's finalize our group questions for the first chapter that was covered by Bethe's fictional story. Rosie will type them up—then we'll vote to accept or reject each one. Then we'll establish a 'Relative Significance Factor' for each question by group average; then, finally, each of us will state our personal 'Credibility-Validation Factor'. Rosie will tote it all up—and we'll be done."

He looked around the room. Some had looked at their watches and groaned. Others, however, laughed. "Great", said Bethe, "Let's get started."

When they were done it had taken over three hours—the final figures were:
• Number of Questions—the professor's initial list of 18 had grown to 28;
• "Relative Significance Factors", established for each question by group average—varied from 1.0 (for many questions) down to .1 and .05;
• "Credibility-Validation Factors"—varied from 1.0 (complete validation) to 0 (no validation).
• The number of separate confirming discoveries were 107, despite only a single numerical count being given for the totality of about fifty Semitic names of slaves in the Brooklyn Papyrus; the Amarna letters with many biblical names; stelae with many names of ancient Hebrew cities; the Ipuwer scroll describing many of the Ten Plagues; the total of all coral-covered chariot wheels discovered; the total of all the skeletal bones of horses and men; etc.

• The final totals of the individual overall validations varied from 73% to 89%, the professor's being 80%. The average group value from their detailed assessment of the overall validation by 21st century data of the biblical Exodus story, including "miracles"—was 80.7%.

It was now after 11, but no one seemed anxious to go. Some were rereading the Bethe-Avi stories, with chuckles and comments.

"I sure enjoyed the military description of sword-spear-shield combat " enthused Rick," where does one learn about such things?" Bethe's laugh was self-conscious, "Our imaginations." She said.

Stewart's comment was measured, thoughtful, "I liked best the escape scene over the undersea-path, it seemed realistic."

"I'm a romantic", said Lanit, "My favorite part was Binami, at the end, remembering his first embrace of Lansel, and his contented, philosophical sum-up of their love and their lives of happiness and fulfillment, from slavery to a promised land, with a great leader, Moses."

There was a short silence. "For me," said Dana? "Oft-times now, I think about this Bible—this small book that's been around for millennia, the foundation of our civilization's Judaic-Christian morality; I think about the Hebrews, the Jews, that tiny sliver of humanity, who've somehow survived for thousands of years despite pogroms and holocausts every few decades—eight million Jews living at the time of the Romans, yet not even twice that today, two thousand years later. One has to wonder about this Bible and of those Israelites!"

Said Serah, "I have to confess also, this journey we've all taken—these monthly sessions, all that we learned—can make a believer of anyone—at least soften to agnosticism anyone who before was a confirmed atheist."

Finally Bethe and Avi got up, "We've got to go." They moved to Professor Barrett their arms outstretched to enclose each other. Wordlessly one by one the others joined—like a reversed "unpeeling" of an artichoke—individuals who had become unified in a sharing of a unique learning experience. Finally all ten were joined in a group-hug. No one spoke for long seconds. Then a female voice murmured. "Unforgettable!"

The year of shared intellectual inquiry had had a unifying effect. An atmosphere of nostalgia hung heavy in the room.

Breinigsville, PA USA
15 February 2011
255649BV00001B/2/P